New Fiction

LIFE'S TREASURES

Edited by

Lucy Jenkins

FOREWORD

When 'New Fiction' ceased publishing there was much wailing and gnashing of teeth, the showcase for the short story had offered an opportunity for practitioners of the craft to demonstrate their talent.

Phoenix-like from the ashes. 'New Fiction' has risen with the sole purpose of bringing forth new and exciting short stories from new and exciting writers.

The art of the short story writer has been practised from ancient days, with many gifted writers producing small, but hauntingly memorable stories that linger in the imagination.

I believe this selection of stories will leave echoes in your mind for many days. Read on and enjoy the pleasure of that most perfect form of literature, the short story.

Parvus Est Bellus.

CONTENTS

SUNDAY
Andrew James Wilsdon

Alone, Alice walked through the large dominating gates of the cemetery, relaxing deep in a tranquil, sombre tornado of thought. The last funeral she had attended had been that of her grandmother. Worcester Road was quiet on this afternoon as she walked slowly through a scene within the theatre of her life, remembering how in the previous summer holiday she had walked down here at night, under the gentle glow of the orange street lights, with her friend, Ben, who had come to meet her from work at the top of the long, sloping road which looked over Bliss Mill. The Common was to her left, partitioned from her by old, black, metal railings; the swings squeaked gently in the breeze, the squeaking a resonant echo of the memories they had been a part of. She turned to face the road and looked to see if it was clear, the road was empty and the air was full of nature's harmony. She crossed with ease, which was strange as this road was always busy, and she continued down the road that steered her for home. Large oak trees dominated the sides of this road (that led downwards to a sharp corner); they rustled, balding and reflecting the ever weakening Autumn sun. The fragile spines of the large leaves led there, naked as they decayed under Alice's feet. Alice walked with her head down, she looked at her feet, her blonde hair strikingly contrasting with the black in which she was adorned. The scene around her was the setting in which she was looking down to the Earth, whilst orbiting within her own confused heaven.

The path had become level, as it had curved around to the bottom of the hill that the town was rested on, and Alice stood at the edge of the path that was next to the local Royal Mail Sorting Office. Around her the town was marinated in history; the latest post arrived where once the train station had brought evacuees. She had to cross the road to a stile, which was the entrance to the isolation of the long footpath that was enclosed by an arching tunnel of trees. Raising her head she looked left and then right. A car came past and she moved quickly away from the edge of the road as she had a flashback from the accident. With hesitation, care and confusion, she slowly made her way across the new unexplored dark black tarmac that still smelt strongly and glistened. The wooden stile was no task for Alice, who climbed it most days when she wanted to retreat from society or was bored. She walked along next to the small stream, that was a canal for the leaves that fell. The sun was pushing harder through the trees as the cover became thicker around her; sunlight fell through the remaining green leaves in direct beams like a laser through smoke. Her feet knew the familiar way as the path led her to an enclosed area in which there were large pieces of old oak resting on the floor that were as ancient as the wood around. Towering overhead, amongst the other trees, was one large Horse Chestnut that grew on the sloping mud side, its roots exposed as it gripped the tender earth.

Alice had stopped a few metres from the pieces of oak. The portrait of the male sat on the largest log seemed to deafen her mind as she stared hypnotically towards him, as he sat staring up into the trees and cried whilst smoking his cigarette, his eyes mirrored the private grief that was killing him within. Alice moved slightly to her left and then stood very still, hidden only by the mask of bramble bush that she looked through. Routinely she took a cigarette from her pocket and she smoked as she had always done here.

She lifted the end of her sleeve past her black leather bracelet to her watch to see what the time was; she then thought of the people, especially her parents at the funeral. She closed her eyes and thought of summer and the music festival with her friends. Freedom, she was filled with freedom along with raging sympathy for the loved friend so close to her, on the large piece of oak that was the one he always sat on. A smile had entered into her thoughts as she thought of those three days of exhilaration, exploration and endless energy. She lifted the cigarette to her mouth and took a long drag and then flicked the ash to the ground.

The congregation stood around the grave and looked down upon the coffin that lay within it. The priest spoke 'Ashes to ashes, dust to dust.' Members of the congregation wept. Young people, who were close friends of the deceased, had gathered, although one had not shown.

The mother stared at the coffin and at the plaque that reflected in the sunlight like someone lost and trying to attract attention. The mother cast away a black leather bracelet into the grave; the coffin echoed with a frightening emptiness as the lamenting leaves blew across the cemetery and then gently fell into the grave.

PUBLIC WARNING
Douglas Bishop

Stop what you are doing, sit down, listen and inwardly digest. This planet is being invaded by aliens from another world!

The last thing I wish to do, is to cause panic but unless we are constantly alert, who knows what will happen?

Observation is the keynote! These beings are beamed down to earth in our likeness, to mingle with us and learn our way of life, then beamed up and debriefed. Why? For what reason? Your guess is as good as mine! Their spacecraft encircle the Earth in a parking orbit. An ability to become invisible and unseen by radar, indicates their superior knowledge.

All is not doom, however, as a large number of these beings have made friends here and do not wish to return to their own planet. Insulation is their safeguard! Have you noticed how many people wear thick-soled trainers? The finest insulation you can get! They just cannot be beamed back. I'm not saying every person wearing trainers are aliens - but be aware of those who *always* wear trainers. Have you noticed the name of some - *hi-tech* - that should make some of you think!

All aliens have a small panel in the centre of their chest. This is their programming device and if meddled with, will self-destruct. Obviously, the way we dress, adequately conceals this from us human beings.

Next time you visit the seaside, observe the number of *people* sitting on the sands, wearing trainers and covered above the waist - no matter how hot the day. All-in-one costumes are not just a new fashion - check at the swimming pool - their panel must always be hidden from view.

Government departments are well aware of what is going on but covered by the Official Secrets Act, everything is hushed-up or totally denied. Now I risk prosecution by telling you that scientists have realised for a long time that underground metal piping has been used by spacecrafts for navigation. Have you noticed, in your area, how gas and water services are being changed to plastic and concrete piping?

Strange, don't you think?

Beware also, people wearing wire-rimmed glasses or carrying metal umbrellas, often when rain is not expected. Remember these make excellent transmitting aerials!

Another giveaway is that none of these aliens have, up to now, been programmed to smile or have any sense of humour. If you are suspicious - crack a joke or tell a funny story. You will then be prepared according to their reaction.

There has not been a case reported of an alien harming a human being, as yet, but take care at all times. There are hundreds of missing persons reported to the police each year. Could some of these have been taken by aliens for experimentation? I would like to think that is not so, but can we be sure?

My colleagues and I have carried out many experiments for protection, with some encouraging results. We have found these aliens are susceptible to copper. A copper-meshed mat has been devised, that has a devastating affect on them. (I will not venture far without mine!)

If confronted by a suspected alien, place your copper-meshed mat on the ground, just in front of you, offer your hand in a greeting manner, he or maybe she will have to step on the mat to shake your hand. Be ready for what may occur.

If he or she is an alien, the copper-mesh will throw their electronic controls into confusion, short circuiting will cause sparks and he or she will quickly disintegrate into a pile of ash. The mesh of your mat will be fused together - ruined, but it has served its purpose. Should he or she turn out to be a fellow human, just explain your behaviour, they will be pleased to have been informed. Pick up you mat and walk away.

You have now all been adequately warned - venture out without your copper-meshed mat - *at your peril!*

THE HEALING TREE
Alan Jones

Alan Jones had grown into adulthood, though remained childlike within; his appearance protruded as a younger man in his late twenties or early thirties - maybe this related to genes, though Alan thought differently. He felt nature was preserving him for something unknown.

Vanity seems to play an important part to many. In some cases, beauty on the outside attracted many more than someone with not so much beauty, though he or she may be gifted.

Alan had worked in all types of employment and at times was treated unkindly, either by employees or some in a higher position. This did not bother Alan a great deal, as he felt that it was all part of learning, also meeting people from all walks of life.

His personal relationships were intense from the beginning, but all ended peacefully.

Having found himself unemployed, though feeling he had something of value to offer, he suddenly withdrew from society, not really understanding why.

Alan was close to his mother; independence was vital and he felt proud of it. A time arrived when Alan found it difficult to go out in the daytime; his mother understood, deciding to do his weekly shopping.

The two years that lay ahead were painful, lonely and filled with constant invasion of privacy by others living in the same household.

Alan happened to by dyslexic. By chance he began drawing, and over the coming year, drew lots of subjects and started to go out more, finding art his main comfort. Overworked, he fell ill and dehydrated, which resulted in him spending a few days in hospital. When fully recovered, he began drawing cartoon characters, also writing stories after which were placed into book format.

Finding himself writing and drawing at a frantic rate, also up all hours, found solace for the first time in his life upon showing his work to an art teacher who remarked that he had a valid talent and found something in art which is difficult to achieve.

This inspired him to work harder. In doing so, he collapsed once again with dehydration. When fully recovered, Alan noticed hair protruding on his chest which resembled the shape of a butterfly; within the year, he started to write poetry, with illustrations to accompany most poems.

Months had passed, and while reading a TV magazine, he noticed a write-up of a Nun sitting in a garden holding a butterfly. The Nun was explaining that the butterfly was the symbol of the poets. Alan hurried to the mirror for a closer look at his chest, truly believing he had been marked by nature. This also cast a fear over him which stopped a returning to misleading ways so as to produce work for many in guidance. Also, to share wisdom was the main aim through his creative projects, believing his commitment was not in vain.

Over the two years that followed, Alan perfected all his projects to publishing standards. Poetry was never meant to overshadow the children's works, though his poetry became noticed and to date has had many poems published for anthologies.

His own illustrated poetry books are completed, also his many children's projects.

Alan found himself drawn closer to nature and though many had not supported him while struggling, he felt the need to help others.

He never set out to seek those who may have needed some type of help, he happened to find himself meeting many by accident or in situations he never would have dared enter. Their difficulties were either emotional or a feeling of lostness within their lives.

He was later to be told that his presence alone was greatly felt. Alan never abused anyone who may have been vulnerable at the time he tried to help.

Feeling complete, though at times alone, he met a female student whom he passed many times. they began talking over issues of the day, and

Alan explained what he was trying to achieve, and later lent his projects to the student.

A week or so later, Alan called to collect his projects and was greeted by the student with delight. Upon leaving, he felt the need to write a poem; all that came to mind was a poem about rewards in an afterlife. This puzzled Alan a great deal.

He delivered the poem and the following day she called to thank him because it meant so much, which puzzled Alan even more. They arranged to have a night out the coming weekend.

Friday morning arrived, Alan decided to go and see his new friend to explain that he would be unable to meet over the weekend as something had come up.

He was greeted by the landlady, who asked him in. After a few minutes, Alan was told that the student had passed away late the previous night, which devastated him, believing that he was at fault. The landlady believed that he was not at fault, as she had been shown the poem and told that it had bought comfort to the student. She had an illness relating to some type of blood disorder which Alan had known nothing about.

Alan had encounters with many and wrote poems over each encounter. These happened to get published, his poetry now taking first place.

Feeling his struggle was nearly over, he happened to be strolling down a park lane, which he did many times. The pathway was lined with many trees not yet in blossoming season. Passing by one particular tree, he felt a sudden jolt. Upon looking upwards, he noticed two tree branches touching one another.

Days had passed. The incident played on Alan's mind so much that he returned to the trees when it was night-time, some force drew him to just one tree; upon touching the tree with both eyes closed, he felt warmth within. Days later, Alan shared his find with close friends. Over a few days, they paid a visit to the tree and to their surprise, felt peace and contentment.

Alan believes nature helped him through many challenges and feels nature will soon release its fear so to share and remain humbled.

When retiring to bed, Alan would have intense dreams that he would remember weeks later in vivid detail. This helped create new works also helped complete unfinished projects.

One particular night when feeling complete, he felt warmth never before felt in both hands. Days later, he happened to touch a friend on a friendly term, which resulted in his friend receiving warmth through their body.

Alan was developing healing abilities. Over a period of time, he found himself meeting many with minor health problems, with both hands began healing waves which involved moving his hands around the body without touching the person. The results were rewarding, as much pain was eased.

He has since helped many and hopes to improve his healing gift. Alan has named this tree *The Healing Tree* and often returns to the tree to pay respects to its power.

As the millennium approaches, those with truth will remain on the periphery of life.

Who is this person Alan Jones?

I am that person . . .

THE STORY OF THE WOOJI FAMILY
W L Brittain

This is the story of the Wooji family who lived in the bottom of an apple tree on a farm belonging to Mr Benjamin.

Mr Wooji, whose name was Sam, lived with his wife Sue and two children named Jilly and Joe.

Now Farmer Ben as he was known to all his friends, let Sam and his family live in the tree because he knew that they would look after the fruit and keep away all nasty insects and things that ate the apples.

Life for Sam was very good because his wife kept the little house clean and tidy whilst Jilly and Joe played around outside. Sam gave himself the job of unpaid guardian of the apples. It was unpaid because Sam did not need any money, food for the family was provided by the fruit that fell from the tree whenever there was a lot of wind. Everything was very well cleaned and cooked before it was eaten, they got all their drink from the juice of the fruit.

Nobody knew how Farmer Ben could tell that the Wooji family lived in the tree because they were so tiny and could hardly be seen. However, he was sure they were there and would look after the fruit on the tree for him.

One day when Sam was marching around the tree checking that everything was in order, he came across Jilly and Joey playing with an apple that was laying on the ground. Now Sam knew that it should not be there because there had been no wind during the night before and nothing unusual had happened to make the apple fall down.

'Oh dear!' he cried, 'that apple should not be there.' He told the children to leave it alone until he had looked at it to try and find out why it had fallen down.

'Oh Daddy' they cried 'we are having so much fun, why must we leave it alone?'
'I'm sorry' said Sam 'but I must examine it to try and find out why it fell down!'

The children ran home to their mother and were very upset that they could not play with the little apple they had found.

'Never mind' said Mum, 'I'm sure that daddy has a good reason for not letting you play with it.'

Sam started to inspect the fallen apple and found that it was full of worm-like holes. This made Sam feel very angry because he knew that if Farmer Ben discovered the apple, he would be very cross and might not let the family stay in their home. Sam looked all around the tree to try and discover what or who had made the holes and suddenly spotted a movement under some dead leaves that were lying near the tree. He quickly ran over to them and found that a family of Eetars had made their home under the leaves.

Now the Eetars were nasty little people who lived on apples, but also made little apples so ill that they fell off the tree before they could grow into big and juicy apples.

Sam and his family decided that they must find a way of getting rid of the Eetars before they did too much damage to the fruit on the tree.

He went home and with his wife and children discussed ways and means of driving the evil wormlike characters away. Sue thought that if they made a lot of noise it might make them go away, so Sam and the children took their little music-making machines over to where the Eetars were living and played them very loudly outside the home. Jilly and Joe said that they would take turns to guard the music machines until the Eetars had gone. One day when Joe was keeping watch and Jilly had gone home for some food, he began to feel sleepy. After all he thought, it is getting a bit boring just sitting here in the sun. He decided to have a nap.

When Jilly returned, Joe was nowhere to be seen and after a quick look around she noticed that the music-makers were also missing.

Oh dear,' she said 'I must go home and get Dad. '

So off she went as fast as her legs would carry her. She ran so fast that when she got home she was out of breath and Mum began to wonder why she had run so fast. When Jilly got her breath back she told Mum about missing Joe and the music-makers. As Dad was not at home when she got there, Mum and Jilly quickly went back to where Joe had last been seen. After having a good look round and still not finding any sign of Joe, they decided to go back and wait for Dad. Sam came home soon after and another search was made. Sue was beginning to get a little bit worried now because she couldn't think where Joe could be. After a long search, they decided that they must return home and get some help. Upon arriving at their little house, they were surprised to find a note pinned to the door. Sam hurried over to read it and became very upset when he read that the Eetars had captured Joe and would not let him go until the Woojis left them in peace.

'What can I do!' thought Sam. 'If I leave the Eetars alone they will ruin all the fruit and Farmer Ben will make me take my home and family away.' He sat down and thought what to do next. I can't let Joe stay in their hands so I must find a way of rescuing him. He gathered the family together and they discussed the best thing to do.

He knew that the Eetars were tiny wormlike creatures and although they were quite harmless to normal children, they could give the Woojis quite a nasty sting.

What Sam did not know was that Joe had been put to sleep by a sting from one of the Eetars and was now lying inside the evil worm's home with his hands tied to a chair to prevent him running away. After a short while, Joe began to come round and started to wonder where he was. He quickly looked around and realised that he was in the Eetar's home and one of the wormlike creatures was guarding him.

He also noticed that the guard was half asleep and was not watching him very well. As Joe was only tied by his hands, he managed to get to his feet and when the guard looked the other way, started to hobble across the room to one of a number of little tunnels that led from the room. Although he did not know quite where he was going, he kept on until he had got right into the tunnel where the guard could not see him. Unfortunately he tripped on a dry leaf and this alerted the guard who, when he saw that Joe was missing called his friends. The Eetars started to look for Joe but he was well into the tunnel and kept running as fast as he could not knowing where he was going. As it turned out Joe had chosen the right tunnel and he soon found himself in the clearing where he had been when he was captured.

Sam and his family had by now decided to go back and make one more search and as they arrived, Joe came out of the tunnel. His Dad quickly untied his hands and after a quick cuddle from Mum, they all ran home.

When they got home, Mum put Joe to bed so that he could have a nice sleep after the terrible ordeal he had been through. Later Joe told his family that the Eetars had crept up on him whilst he had been dozing and put him to sleep with a nasty sting. They had then carried him and the music-makers into their home and tied him to a chair. Dad then said that it was time for them all to have a good rest before deciding what to do next . . .

Mum was first up next morning and she began to get the family's breakfast ready before Sam and the children got out of bed. After a meal of fried apple and apple juice, Dad went outside to see if there were any Eetars about, but found that they had all gone home.

Later that morning the children went out to play and got quite a nasty surprise. Although the wormlike creatures were not about, they had left several little apples lying around, which they had half-eaten.
'Daddy,' they cried 'come here quickly and look at these little apples.'
When Dad saw the damaged fruit he became very upset and decided that he would have to do something about the Eetars before Farmer Ben saw the fruit and decided that Sam and his family could not do their job properly and tell them to leave their little house.

He had another talk with Jilly, Joe and Sue and they decided that the only way to get rid of the evil little people would be to try and block up the holes leading to their home and try to drive the Eetars away.

Later that night when it was very dark, they called on their friend Charlie Squirrel and told him of their idea to get rid of the Eetars

Charlie was very interested, because he had also had some trouble with the little people and would be pleased to see them go away.

It was decided between them that Charlie Squirrel and his friends would drop nuts around the openings to the Eetars homes so that Sam and his family could roll them into the openings and block them up.

This was working very well until the Eetars heard the noise and came running out to see what was going on. As fast as the squirrels and Woojis pushed the nuts into the holes, the Eetars were pushing them out again. After a while Sam and friends realised that this way was not going to work because there were far more Eetars than they realised.

Sam's family and the squirrels began to get very tired and decided that they would have to go home for a rest. Home they all went, feeling very sad - whilst the Eetars danced with joy. This did not please Charlie Squirrel and made him all the more determined to get rid of them.

With all his friends, Charlie and the Wooji family had a meeting and talked about other ways to get rid of the Eetars. After a long discussion the squirrels came up with an idea. If Sam and his family could make a lot of noise so that the worm-like people would come out to find out what was going on, the squirrels would drop acorns on them from the trees above and try to drive them away. They didn't want to hurt them but just make them go away and leave the fruit alone. This they all agreed to do as long as no harm came to the Eetars.

Early the next morning, Sam and Sue together with Joe and Jilly crept round to the back of the Eetar's home and began to bang old pieces of tin together to make a noise. Charlie Squirrel and his friends waited in the trees above ready to drop the acorns when the Eetars came out. To the surprise of Sam and his family, instead of running away as they had hoped, the Eetars ran back into their homes again. This so upset Charlie and friends that they came down from the tree and started digging into the tunnels to try and get at the Eetars. When they had made an opening Sam and Joe went into the home and tried to drive the evil people out. They did not take Sue and Jilly with them in case they all got caught again. However, when they got inside, there was no sign of the Eetars and Sam began to wonder where they were. They kept going further and further into the home and suddenly heard the sound of singing.

'Quiet Joe,' said Sam. The two of them began to creep quietly towards the sound of the singing and to their surprise they came into a large open space where all the Eetars had gathered and were celebrating their victory by dancing around the music-makers that they had stolen from Joe when they captured him.

'What is going on Dad?' said Joe.

'I don't know,' said Dad 'but I think we had better go back to where Sue and Jilly are waiting before we do anything else.'

Back they went. There was no need to be quiet because the evil people were making so much noise they wouldn't have heard them. When they got outside again, they found Sue and Jilly and all ran home.

Charlie Squirrel called round to see them and asked what they had found out. When Sam told him, he was very annoyed and went off to talk with his friends again about ways that would get rid of the nasty people for good.

Together they decided that if they blocked up all the little holes except one, they could drive them out by filling the opening with smoke. They called Joe and his family out and told them of their plan and it was agreed that they would start right away, whilst the Eetars were singing and dancing. The squirrels dropped lots of acorns to the ground and the Woojis began to roll them into the openings as fast as they could. They then decided that if they made a little fire and created a lot of smoke, they could blow the smoke into the hole they had left open and hope to drive the Eetars out that way - when the smoke got into their eyes so that they could not see. They built a little fire with twigs and other dry bits of material and when it was well alight they piled green leaves on top to make the smoke.

The smoke got thicker and the wind started to blow it into the little opening and all the friends waited to see what would happen. They began to think that the plan hadn't worked because nothing happened. However after a little wait the first of the Eetars came running out of the hole with their eyes streaming with water and coughing badly. Sam noticed that some of them carried little banners saying that they would go away if Sam and his friends left them alone. This pleased Sam and his friends because that was all they wanted. the Eetars agreed to move their home to the other side of the farm where there were no fruit trees and never come back again.

When they had gone, Sam and Joe waited until the smoke had cleared before going into the home to make sure they were all gone. After a good search they found nothing only their music-makers which the Eetars had left behind, and although they were a little damaged by smoke - they still worked.

The worm people's home was sealed up to stop them going back and Sam and his family left to live in peace with the squirrels who had helped them so well . . .

RELATIVELY REM
Caroline Sammout

'Jen, wake up!' Jerking upright from her sudden brief slumber, Jennifer sighed heavily.
'You're at it again Jen', whispered her colleague Sophie.
'I can't help it, I haven't had a good night's sleep since I moved into that house!'
'Probably the new surroundings' Sophie replied.
'Yeah!' Jennifer answered and knuckled back down to work.

As the day drew to a close, Jennifer sat in silence staring at the blank TV screen. She felt slightly uneasy and even though it was very late she was reluctant to retire, instead she decided that another cup of coffee may relieve her desire to sleep. Settling back on the sofa, cupping her mug of coffee in her hands Jennifer wearily looked over to the clock on the wall.
'Ugh, 3 o'clock' she thought, as she sipped her drink.
The late night chill began to tease her skin and as she shivered, decided to give into the exhaustion that filled her body. Finally, after dragging her heavy limbs up the stairs and into the bedroom, she flopped down onto the bed covering herself with her dressing gown. Immediately sleep overcame her.

In the distance Jennifer could see a figure, squinting, she tried to identify the stranger.
'Please help' it pleaded, holding out a hand. Jennifer tried to approach but as she moved closer the figure drifted further away.
'Who are you?' she asked.
'Please help; it repeated *'just once - that's all'.*
Jennifer awoke abruptly and stumbled from her bed, she staggered into the bathroom and took a refreshing shower.

Arriving at work, Jennifer was greeted by Sophie, 'Good God Jen, you look awful!'
'Good morning to you too Sophie!' Jennifer replied as she slumped down behind her desk.

'What's wrong Jen, are you still not sleeping?'

Jennifer shook her head, 'I'm being plagued by the same dream every bloody night', she sighed rubbing her eyes.

'What dream?' enquired Sophie.

'Oh, I don't know' she shrugged 'just some person asking for help and then going *'just once, just once'* all the bloody time'.

Sophie raised her eyebrows 'Oh, I see'.

Jennifer gave Sophie a glance and grinned, 'Oh, don't worry, it's probably like you said yesterday, all new surroundings and such, they'll pass'.

'You know what you need, don't you Jen?' whispered Sophie.

'What's that then?' Jennifer asked.

'A man!'

Jennifer sniggered and settled down to her work.

Jennifer could hardly keep her eyes open when she arrived home, 'I'll just sit down for five minutes' she thought and fell into the sofa. Predictably what she thought would be a little rest turned out to be long needed sleep. Whilst drifting into deeper slumber, she was overcome by a beautiful scent and a feeling of complete peace. Suddenly her surroundings were familiar. Again in the distance a figure reached out *'Please help. Just once, that's all I ask!'*

This time Jennifer slept on and the dream continued. The figure approached her; for the first time Jennifer could see the face of this unknown stranger. It was a woman, she was beautiful but her eyes showed sadness and pain.

'Please help me, I cannot rest. I need to look upon the face of my child. I need her to know I've always loved her. I never gave up. Please can you help me?'

The woman led Jennifer into the spare bedroom but it was still in its former glory. Antique furniture adorned the room and family photos adorned the walls. Lilies filled several vases and Jennifer realised that this was the scent she was familiar with when she slept. The woman pointed to the corner of the room *'All you need is beneath this floor'* she said *'I had to hide it. They didn't know I saw her. I always loved her. I want her to have what is hers, then I can rest. Please, please will you help me?'*

Jennifer's eyes shot open and without thinking she ran into the spare room. Dodging the unpacked boxes she made her way over to the corner that the woman had shown her. Immediately she began pulling back the old red carpet which covered the patched-up floorboards. After searching for something to pry open the boards she set to work pulling at the old but still sturdy wood.

Suddenly the floorboard was free. Underneath covered in dirt and dust lay a sheet, Jennifer paused then forced her hands to remove it. Beneath the sheet was an old-fashioned box. Slowly she picked it up and carried it carefully into her room. She felt slightly wary and her breathing became heavy, but curiosity won her over and she set about opening the box. What she saw inside filled her with emotion, there were many letters, pencil drawings, old photos and a gold locket. As Jennifer read through the letters it became clear why the woman in her dream was suffering such torment.

As a young girl she had fallen pregnant but when the baby was born, to save shame falling on the family, it was snatched from her breast and handed over to a childless, well-to-do couple.

The woman's quest, to find her child became her life. She wrote numerous letters intended to be passed on to the child but when she tracked-down her daughter, she knew she could not destroy the good life this young girl now knew with the family who obviously loved her. Instead she would sit for hours outside the house where her daughter lived in the hope of catching a glimpse of her. She had even sketched pictures of the house just to feel close to the child.

At this point a feeling of familiarity began to fill Jennifer's head, she placed a hand over her mouth, tears welled in her eyes.
'I know this place,' she murmured. She continued to look through the box of memories and pulled out the numerous photos. The woman looked younger in her dreams, but the pictures showed her more aged and more familiar to Jennifer.
'Oh my God!' she exclaimed.

With daytime well underway, she quickly repacked the box and took it downstairs. Still in her previous day's working clothes Jennifer raced to her car and set off at speed.

Arriving at her destination she made her way toward the front door where, taking a deep breath, she knocked.

An elderly woman answered, Jennifer smiled, 'Hello Gran'.

'Hello Jenny love' Gran replied, giving her a warm hug, 'come on in, I'll make some tea.'

'No we can't, I need you to come with me!'

'Oh, why's that then dear?' Her Grandma asked.

'I'll tell you on the way. You haven't seen my new house, so you can stay for lunch.'

'Alright then, but let me get my coat.'

As she waited, Jennifer noticed a vase of lilies in the hall and felt a shiver run down her spine.

'Right, I'm ready love, and make sure you don't drive too fast, I'm getting on now, eighty-eight you know'.

Jennifer smiled as she helped her Grandma into the car and headed for home.

After the grand tour of the house, Jennifer served her Gran a cup of tea and sat next to her on the sofa.

'Gran, do you remember when you found out you were adopted. Did you ever try to find your natural mother?'

'Where on earth did that question come from Jenny?' came her Gran's surprised reply.

'Well, it's something that I've been wondering about.'

Her Grandma shook her head 'If only I could have love, but she died you see and the only thing I could do was just get on with my life. I do wonder about her sometimes. I heard she died alone.'

Jennifer held her Gran's hand 'What is it Jenny love, is something wrong?'

'It's such a long story Gran, but I have something that belongs to you. It's time to put the past to rest.'

Jenny regained her composure and handed the box to her Gran. Gently, she helped her Grandma to relive many missing years. Overcome with emotion and in tears, Jennifer comforted her.

The box of secrets was at last with it's rightful owner, questions answered at last and peace found.

There were no more dreams after that day. As Jennifer arranged yet another bunch of lilies on the corner unit in her spare room, she dedicated them to the past and felt a sense of calm and an encouraging reassurance that the once-tortured soul was now at rest.

BREAKING UP THE OZONE
Terry Ramanouski

People were running scared. The whole of America was affected. People suffered from cancer of the skin and eyes, tumours, heat-stroke, breathlessness. The rich had left, upped and gone to England, France and Spain. Most of the general public had gone underground to catacombs, the army had dug out two years ago. The people were real mad at the government for causing this catastrophe, although they were as much to blame, one and all. Just like everyone else the world over. Yes, the ozone has gone! The top scientists said it cannot come back. It is gone forever and will keep shrinking and shrinking until no more. It was comical in a way. Everyone on the street had to go around wearing white cotton suits or overalls. Lawyers, bank managers, shop owners, street cleaners, tramps, each wearing masks with built-in sunglasses. The police had helmets with visors. It was imperative to keep the ultra violet out.

There was to be an international meeting in Geneva and talk of arrest of government American politicians. What would they do? Absolutely nothing! People would have to leave eventually as the sea was rising. Thousands upon thousands had been evacuated from the coast. The scientists stated that Canada and South America were next. The ozone was paper thin and once that happens, the whole American continent would have to be evacuated. Where could they go? The politicians would be alright and the rich. But what about the poor ordinary people? They would be left to the elements for sure.

Yes, it was looking very, very bad! Experts said that in a couple of weeks the whole continent would be engulfed by the Pacific and Atlantic oceans. It would be no use going to the mountains. What then? What would you live on - fresh air! Ha! Ha! . . . that would be a laugh because there will be none, plus you would roast anyway!

The temperature was now one hundred degrees and rising. The Jehovah's Witnesses were spouting their usual flim flam that God punched a hole right through the sky with his fist to punish the fornicators, murderers, corrupt politicians, the vain, the greedy, adulterers, prostitutes, child abusers. The list was endless. they kept on saying this on their own television station. Also on the streets, calling it the new Babylon and people were going to suffer. Repent your sins now while you can. The TV stations had hundreds of thousands of callers, but understandably only hundreds could be dealt with. They did not have the manpower or phones. So most of the population had to sweat it out, as they say! The news on TV and the papers were saying Jehovah's Witnesses should shut up, as many people were scared enough.

The more sensible ones asked if God has punched a hole in the sky to punish people, wicked people, why should decent people suffer? What kind of God is that? It does not make any sense, does it? Anyway, the temperature rose to one hundred and six in the shade. Then the newsflashes 'Get out while you can! Get on a boat, ship, anything. Best of all, make a raft. Take water in plastic bottles, glass if you can. Tinned food with tin openers. Warm clothing, soft drinks and biscuits - no alcohol as that would dehydrate you.

Because there will be so many people at sea it will be weeks, maybe months, before getting to somewhere safe which offered sanctuary.

Do not delay . . . Do it now!

The seas are closing-in fast. Good luck!

Within three days the American continent was under water. Millions of people and animals drowned. Other countries helped but with two hundred and fifty million American citizens, not counting Canada central, and the southern part of the continent, it was an impossible task with so many people. Hundreds of thousands died at sea. It was a terrible ordeal.

Now it was over . . . The American continent was gone.

Whose turn was it next, Africa, India, Japan or maybe Great Britain?

The seas were rising dramatically . . . Was this the end?

THE SHOP
N K Todd

Cobwebs hung around Zack's head like tattered locks as he surveyed the ghostly silence of the cramped shop. Light cast by an oil lamp showed a couple of stuffed armchairs, but no merchandise, nor proprietor. Brushing aside the cobwebs, Zack turned, as from the shadows the figure of a man appeared.

Zack watched in amazement, as the short ugly figure loped over and dropped into one of the armchairs, declaring 'I'm Anton, gentleman of fortune, who are you?'

Zack claiming the chair opposite, looked into the wizened face, and told him he had been an apprentice to a jeweller, but had just purchased suitable premises to start his own business.

'Good choice, many a fine lady I've caught with the odd trinket,' Anton said with a gleam in his eyes. 'Mind I once relieved a gentleman of a fine opal after which my fortune took a downward turn, but opals can be strange baubles, don't suit some. Still if I owned more than this fine opal, I could just see myself with a shop, surrounded by precious stones and costly trinkets, think of the ladies I could catch,' Anton said, with a faraway look in his eyes.

Zack being of a shy nature, could not imagine a lady fine or otherwise, smiled. Secretly he admired Anton's easy way of life but, being of a more cautious nature, settled for a steadier route to his goal. His shop was only the beginning of an empire, full of the world's glittering gems. No rocky road of chance for him.

Shaking out of his muse, he noticed there was still no sign of the shop's owner, so Zack bade his companion a 'Good evening,' and strolled out of the shop.

Walking along the alley, hands in pockets, his fingers felt a hard object in his pocket, bringing it out, his eyes fell upon the finest opal he had ever seen, his shocked eyes looked back at the shop front, a weathered sign read

Dream Exchange'.

CHOSEN ONE
Mabel Helen Underwood

He couldn't really hear it because there was no sound to hear, only a deep throbbing which came from below him.

Panic-stricken, he scrambled up between the rocks, slipping on gravel at every step. Jutting ledges tore his fingers as he grasped them. Acrid fumes hurt his throat as he gasped for breath. His heart thumped painfully.

At last he reached the ridge and breathed cooler air.

He could see no path down on the other side - only a steep slope of small fragments of lava, like shale. Leaving the ridge that way would mean sliding, rolling, crashing to his death. He had to go on, stumbling round the rim of the great hole, towards the group of tourists far away on the other side of the crater.

Horror filled his mind. They were following the guide over the lip and down inside the crater. Laughing, excited, they couldn't have felt the throbbing.

It was too late for him, but they might have a chance if only he could warn them. He tried to yell but his voice had no power.

He stumbled towards a gap in the rocks, his chest heaving. He held on to a boulder, pitted and rough, and looked into the volcano's crater. It looked normal. No gaping hole, no hot lava boiling up, not even a sign of smoke. Had he panicked for nothing?

The strength which fear had given him began to ebb away and his legs felt like the milky jelly they'd made him eat. Was he really going to live? He looked down into the crater, as deep as a skyscraper and wide enough to engulf a stadium. All was still. He must have imagined the thudding throb beneath the rock he'd been sitting on. As he turned away his foot dislodged a small piece of hard lava which went spinning and bouncing from ledge to ledge into the depths below him. He watched, fascinated, until it struck the pebble-strewn floor with a hollow booming sound, as if it had landed on the stretched skin of a giant drum.

Fear clutched his heart again. Motionless, he waited for the noise to cease. Could the floor of the crater, just a skin of thin hardened lava, stand the vibration, or would a rent appear, giving him a glimpse of the white-hot core of the volcano before it erupted and killed him - and the tourists? Would tourists of the future see the blackened shell of his body as he'd seen the shell of the dog caught in the ruins of Pompeii?

He heard, faintly, squeals of nervous laughter. A wisp of smoke blew across the crater below him. The guide was at it again - blowing cigarette smoke under the hot rock and bringing out a cloud of vapour, trying to frighten the tourists. How many times had he seen that since Vesuvius had cast its spell on him?

He glanced downwards again. A glow seemed to give unusual brightness to the bottom of the crater. Rocks stood out, dark against the paler floor littered with fallen pebbles.

The tourists - a small group - were climbing, one by one, out of the crater and disappearing over its rim. They'd be stumbling and slipping, he knew, down the path of gravelly lava, perhaps stopping to empty their shoes. Their bus would be waiting half-an-hour's struggle below the top of the cone. He must follow them. Yet it was good to be alone again with the volcano after that spell in hospital.

One last look into the crater, he thought.

The glow, deep down below him, really was brighter. It wasn't - it couldn't be - the rays of the sun. The deepest part of the hole should be in shadow by now. Why was it shining like an inverted cone of light?

Then he felt it again - that deep, silent, throbbing sensation. He clung to a boulder, his heart racing.

Out of the crater there rose a bright mist, swirling beneath him, warm, exciting.

This must be the end, he thought - strangely pleasant, with memories of his boyhood. Memories returned at the end, he'd heard. He used to breathe deeply when the dentist was giving him gas. He was afraid the tooth might be pulled before he was unconscious, wanting it to be over quickly and then wake up. Well, he wouldn't wake up this time. He breathed more deeply.

Why wasn't he unconscious already? Perhaps he was, or delirious. He was seeing things. The mist was swirling into bright star-shapes, glowing like molten metal, wheeling up the inside of the crater towards him. Then the mist had gone completely and he was looking at a semicircle of red-hot stars, about twice his own height, quite still below him. He could feel their heat on his face and had to shield his eyes.

The throbbing in his ears began again and this time it seemed to mean something. It made sense. The thoughts his mind were picking up were, he knew, coming from those incandescent creatures in front of him.

'We will not harm you.'

His mind translated the thoughts into words which calmed his agitation. He replied with his own thoughts.

'Who are you? Where've you come from?'

'Now? From the crater where we waited. But our home is a planet orbiting another sun. Your world's most powerful telescope might show you our sun.'

He gasped.

'Then you're . . . from Outer Space! Extra-terrestrial beings!'

The answer came clearly to his mind.

'From *your* Outer Space, yes. We have been waiting until your mind was attuned to ours. We have been patient.'

'Then that was why I was so fascinated by Vesuvius - why I couldn't keep away?'

'You came because we were calling you.'

'But . . . have you been living *in* the volcano? How've you survived?'

He felt amusement in the thoughts he received - an impression, almost, of laughter. If they could laugh.

'Do Earthmen think there can be no life except on worlds where conditions resemble theirs?'

'That's true - for most of them. But I've never been so sure of it. You see, I'm a scientist - not a distinguished one, just a teacher. The kids in my classes used to love outrageous ideas.'

But he'd never dare to tell them about this. Some would talk, and then where would he end up? He couldn't bear to go there again - kind though they'd been.

A new wave of enquiry passed to him.

'What about the nature of your species?'

He almost laughed.

'They'd put me away again.'

'You will be believed. The power we give you will overcome all men.'

'Me? Power? But that's not me. I just want to be left alone to study and teach. And visit volcanoes.'

'Quite. No other man would have remained sane. But we have conditioned you.'

'Why? What d'you want me to do?'

'Save your world.'

'Save . . .! From what? I can't save it from you now.'

'You must save it from itself. Earth is heading towards self-destruction. Only you can prevent it. If you will do our bidding Earth will survive. That is why we have come.'

'Well, I know we're in a bad way. I do follow the news. But what can I do? I'm only mortal, and just an ordinary one.'

'As we pass from your sight you will be given the power to govern all men. Then we will direct you.'

He cried aloud in dismay.

'Why me?'

The reply seemed to burn into his brain.

'You are the Chosen One. Prepare to rule the world.'

There was a roar as if the volcano erupted, but only the star-shapes rose slowly out of the crater, dazzling as the sun. They hovered, changed into bright swirling mist, became transparent and disappeared.

A feel of exultation filled him. He had been chosen to lead the world! The star-shapes had gone but had left him their wisdom. He could never fail.

He walked to where he could look out over the city spread below him. His eyes were as keen as an eagle's and he saw, past the group of fearful tourists huddled below, all round the great Bay of Naples - thousands and thousands of people staring at the cone of Vesuvius where the star-shapes had glittered away - everyone staring up to where he stood on the highest point.

Unbelievable confidence overwhelmed his mind and body. He was omnipotent here on Earth. The creatures had spoken truly.

Their demand came, clear and compelling.

'Throw yourself down from the pinnacle of the mountain. We will bear you up. They will see and believe - and obey. Nations will unite at your command. Out over the gulf, oh Chosen One of Earth!'

He raised his arms to where the swirling incandescence had disappeared. Power contracted his muscles and then released them like a spring. Over the highest slope he flew and then plummeted towards the rocks below.

'Pauvre 'nomo,' they said as they looked at the shattered body. 'How frightened he must have been.'

GIVERNY
Peter Sowter

'Good morning Madam, can I help you?' the assistant said.

'Yes, I certainly hope so,' replied the thirty-something woman determinedly. 'I bought this eyeshadow last week and my best friend tells me, the shade doesn't suit me one bit.'

'Well Madam,' began Claudette, 'you have lovely eyes, they are possibly one of your best features and only need a slight emphasis!' 'Perhaps,' she continued, 'if you were to augment that shade with another, close to it, your friend would appreciate the subtlety of the Yves St Laurent range, after all it is French! Madam.'

A good start for Monday morning, thought Claudette, as the woman went off content with the extra eyeshadow and a lipstick as well.

It turned out to be a very good morning indeed, when she had a telephone call from her sales manager at Head Office, to tell her that she had won the contest for the best sales figures in Scotland. The prize being a long weekend in Paris, Claudette L'Argent, whose father was French, was overjoyed.

Claudette, 'Claudie' to her friends, was 19, not beautiful, but decidedly pretty, about 5'4", with natural, wavy, reddish-brown hair. A wide brow, hazel eyes flecked with green, a small but straight nose, a generous mouth with a ready smile. Everybody liked Claudette.

She left school with 2 'A' levels, one in Art, her favourite subject and the other in French, putting off a decision about university. Her boyfriend Stuart was a trainee manager at Arnott's, the large department store in Sauchiehall Street. He knew of a vacancy on the Yves St Laurent counter, she applied and obtained the position. After a three-week intensive training course at the Head Office, Claudette soon settled in, becoming an efficient demonstrator and saleswoman.

As the year progressed Claudette's parents urged her to think about going to university. She was quite content with her job, it was going well. Stuart was around, she had some cash to spend and to study for a degree in French, Art, not considered viable enough by her family, seemed drab and boring.

Claudette arranged with Head Office to have a week of her annual holiday tacked onto the weekend she had won. In Paris, she spent the time in the Louvre and the Musée d'Orsay, strolling sometimes along the Rive Gauche and even managed to sketch a little in the Place de Tertre.

When the weekend was over, Claudette took the train from the Gare St Lazare to Vernon, some 50 kilometres north west of Paris, where her penfriend Nicole lived with her parents. Nicole was at the Sorbonne, but would be home later in the week. Nicole's parents begged her to stay and seeing her sketches of Paris, suggested that she use Nicole's bicycle to explore the local countryside.

Each day she cycled around and found some location to sketch. The weather was clear and sunny, warm but not too hot. After a day or so she wished that she had brought her paints, as a particular setting attracted her. In the foreground there was a river, she thought it might be the Epte, across on the opposite bank a glimpse of a farmhouse amid the leafy trees. It was while she was drawing that a voice in her ear startled her,

'Vous dessinez très bien Mademoiselle.'

She turned to see a man about forty years old, with a longish face, black curly hair and beard, rather handsome, she thought.

'Merci Monsier, on fait ce que l'on peut,' she replied.

He told her that the pencil did not do justice to the scene and she explained that her paints were far away in Scotland.

Later in the day after she had the picnic lunch that Nicole's mother Madame Maffre, had prepared, and was drawing again, he reappeared, this time with a parcel of sorts under his arm and she noticed that his clothes were somewhat old-fashioned. Perhaps he was a writer or something similar, rusticating in the countryside.

In the parcel which he carefully unwrapped, after telling her how pleased he was that she was still there, were two blank canvases on stretchers and a shallow box containing a palette, assorted paints and brushes. He finally persuaded her to accept them, saying that they were very old and would have been thrown away any day now. The following day, she quickly transferred her sketch to one of the canvases and was painting furiously when 'Curly' as she now called him to herself, appeared.

He was excited by her painting and could not prevent himself from suggesting colouring, shadow and light effects. At some other time she would have perhaps considered him a nuisance, eventually handing back the paints and moving off. Now she fell in with his ideas and towards the late afternoon the painting was more or less complete. While he was helping her clean the brushes, he suggested that tomorrow she visit the famous gardens in the nearby village, 'a small admission fee,' he said. If he could get away he might see her there and would point out one or two special scenes for painting. When she asked, he said,

'Yes, I was a painter once.'

The next day at the garden, she was surprised at the number of people there, but once inside strolling around, looking at the house and the garden they did not seem so obtrusive. She had brought the other canvas and was looking for somewhere to paint, when he came by her side.

'Come, let's go to the Clos Normond, the water garden.' And he led her through the tunnel under the road and out by the Japanese Bridge, where they gazed down on the water lilies. For a moment she remembered Le Bassin aux Nympheas in the Musèe d'Orsay.

'Over there,' he said suddenly, 'that's the scene, I never did paint it, now you can paint it for me.'

He went off for a moment and miraculously returned with an easel. Soon the painting was in full flow. Claudette had never felt so competent. He was constantly at her elbow, advising, correcting.

People stopped to stare at her work, spoke to her. They called to one another, 'Come look at this pretty girl, how well she paints,' completely ignoring him. After her picnic lunch, he rejoined her and they worked hard through the afternoon until the gardens were closing. As she was ready to mount her cycle, the canvas and paints strapped to the carrier, he said, 'Au revoir ma chere Mademoiselle' and kissed her hand. She never saw him again.

The next day she searched and enquired of him to no avail. She had asked no questions of him and he none of her, they were like ships passing in the night, an apt expression, thought Claudette, who had read it somewhere.

Claudette was delighted with the garden painting, she knew it was good. That night she slept fitfully, once she awoke with a start, sensing his presence there in her room, but reassured herself that it was just a dream and smiling softly she went back to sleep.

After the weekend with Nicole and her friends, she returned home to Glasgow. She had made up her mind to become an artist, in spite of everybody's advice to the contrary. The garden painting she sent to the Royal Academy for a chance in the Summer Exhibition. A little more than a week later, she received a letter asking her to come to the Royal Academy in Piccadilly. As she was escorted through the Friends Room to a far door, her nerves almost overcoming her, she felt her hand squeezed and a calmness engulfed her. The door opened revealing a long room, well-lit from the tall windows overlooking the courtyard. Three men were chatting around a painting, set up on an easel by a window. One of the men immediately came over to greet her.

'Thank you for coming all this way, Miss Money,' he said, 'we are most intrigued with the painting you sent us. This is Anthony Bingham from Sotheby's a noted expert on French Impressionists and Sir Charles Appleby, one of the Summer Exhibition selectors. My name is John Stanford and quite frankly, we don't know what to make of this painting. Could we first look through your portfolio, which we requested you bring with you?'

They looked at her drawings and water colours for some time, then they turned to her. This time, Sir Charles spoke

'Leaving aside this painting, pointing at the easel, for a moment, I would be pleased, if you are interested, to offer you a place at the Royal College of Art this autumn. Claudette felt the tears well up into her eyes, it was what she had always wanted, a chance to study Art. She couldn't speak, just nodded and sat down fishing for her handkerchief. She wasn't aware of anyone ordering it, but a tray of coffee had been brought in. As she began to feel better they chatted to her, and amongst themselves. Then John Stanford said with a smile,

'Now that your future has been decided, at least for a couple of years, let's talk about this painting you sent to us. First of all, I am right, aren't I, that this is a view in the garden at Giverny?'

Claudette nodded in reply.

'The canvas, the stretchers, are about 100 years old, the paint looks recent though its chemical composition is old, it might have been recently cleaned though.' Following a brief pause, he continued, 'The signature is a little obscured on one or two letters, because the paint colour has merged with the background. We are inclined to believe this painting is genuine.'

'Of course, it's genuine,' retorted Claudette, 'I painted it!' and she explained how she acquired the canvas and paints.

'If you painted it then,' Anthony Bingham broke in, 'why did you sign it Claude Monet?'

Claudette couldn't help herself, she burst out laughing,

'I didn't,' she said, 'I signed my name Claudie Money!'

THE HOUSE
Caroline Elizabeth Ashton

I could never have prepared myself enough as I steeled myself around the final bend in the meandering lane. I knew it would still be there years later. Houses like that never alter beyond recognition - they are solid, stone-built, eternal. I crossed the dirt-track lane, my quickening pace propelled me closer to my destination - and there it was. Nestling deep within a thicket of ancient elm trees, the house was still standing. I was horrified by its dilapidated appearance. This was hardly the beautiful safe haven of my childhood.

The once-manicured lawns were almost waist-high with rye grass and the neat flower beds totally obliterated. After climbing over the fallen, broken pieces of wood that were once the gate, I carefully picked my way along the bramble-strewn path towards the front door.

Looking upwards, my eyes caught a glimpse of sunlight which was reflected off a shard of broken glass hanging like an icicle off the top window casing. This was the only piece of glass in the entire window - the rest must have been in pieces on the bedroom floor. The dark, gaping holes remaining in the broken window frames were like bleak, sad eyes in a pale, wan face. It broke my heart to see it thus.

As I took my final steps on approach, I became aware that my head was cocked to one side - I was listening for the 'once-usual' bark of Flossie. My long-forgotten habit was still deeply ingrained sixty years later. Of course there was no such noise of barking dog, only the chirruping of sparrows within the overgrown hawthorn hedge broke the still, clear afternoon.

Tentatively my hand went towards the rusty handle on the door. There was no need to knock as the place was long deserted and uninhabitable in its present rundown state. The door creaked open noisily under the slight pressure of my fingers; fragments of dark green paint fluttered onto the flags below. I was now inside the house of my childhood.

Years ago, I would have been overwhelmed by the delicious aroma of Grandma's bread baking in the Aga stove - but there was nothing now. Had the roof and windows all been fully intact, then the dank smell of mould would have invaded my nostrils, but with all the excess ventilation, only the smell of the hawthorn blossom carried in by the wind remained.

Creeping (as I had also done over sixty years earlier) into Grandma's forbidden front parlour, I could almost feel her annoyance. Children were not allowed entry, so all the more reason for cousin George and I to want to sneak in. My rheumy eyes took in the shabby state. Great gaps had been ripped in the faded wallpaper revealing bouquets of once-crimson roses several layers below the top pale-green woodchip. Other torn patches in the strata of paper exposed the cascades of lilac blossom, so faded by years of exposure, that they were almost white. There were half-inch deep craters in the crumbling plaster and the ceiling wallpaper hung down in great tongues. The large open fireplace which used to host a magnificent log-fuelled fire in winter was now rendered useless. Soot-coated bricks had fallen out of the chimney, bringing down a pile of dust and soot in their wake, covering the tiled hearth with a thick, grimy, black film. On the once highly polished mahogany mantleshelf, the china dogs had now abandoned their silent vigil over their domain. They always sat at either end of the mantleshelf and were my grandmother's pride and joy. As a girl, they always seemed so high up - George had to lift them down for me to stroke - ah, but now everything had gone. There were many indentations in the patchy lino where the heavy furniture legs had left their circular footprints. The bureau, the dresser, the grandfather clock - they had all left their insignia and I was proud to remember where everything had once been, so very long ago.

TALKIES
Shirley Sammout

Lily loved her work, it kept her close to her heroes. As usherette in a small picture house she was abreast of all the new films and romantic male leads. There he was on the screen, Sebastian, the latest star from America. So handsome, a dark curl touched his forehead giving a childlike appeal, yet his virile body and sexy smile had all the women swooning in the aisles. Lily was no exception, she adored Sebastian, often daydreaming of riding into the sunset, 'sweet nothings' whispered in her ears. Giggling, she wondered if his sweet little moustache would tickle during a kiss. She could only imagine his voice, as these were the days of the silent movie.

After selling her refreshments, she stood at the rear of the picture house watching the film, it was so exciting, especially at the turn of the week when a new film was screened. However, she didn't want this week to end, it could be weeks before a Sebastian film was shown again.

The building was empty, the four usherettes took turns to clean the picture house. The mess was never too bad, two would stay behind and it was cleared in no time. Each was paid an extra few pennies each time their turn came round, which proved handy at the month's end buying a few luxuries especially on an early Bioscope-type film magazine. This month's contained Sebastian, many bedroom walls would be adorned with the carefully cut-out picture, including Lily's.

Dust sheets were thrown over the more expensive seats in the raised boxes on each side of the screen and occasionally sent out to be laundered. Sally shared Lily's shift today, before the afternoon performance, the sheets were removed. The manager left instruction that today was laundry day, Lily was to take them out to the van waiting in front of the building. The rolled sheets were quite heavy as she heaved one under each arm. Carefully she descended the twenty steps which led from the foyer to the pavement below, daydreaming a descent down the grand staircase into the ballroom. Lily was no dainty, tutored film star, she was just Lily and known to be slightly clumsy. She raised her head to look for the van driver but he was nowhere in sight, probably somewhere flirting with Sally. Eyes diverted towards the laundry van, Lily missed her footing and as she stumbled, let go of the dust sheets. They bounced onto the step, then again and again and quickly unrolled; twenty steps completed the rolls lay flat. Lily descended as quickly as possible but with no Sally around to help, folding the sheets was hard work.

Lily stopped, gathering the covers, as she did two highly polished boots glinted up at her.

'Can I be of any assistance?' the wearer asked.

Her gaze turned towards the voice. Towering at least a foot above her five-foot frame was the most good-looking man she had ever seen. There in the flesh, in soldier's uniform, was the double of Sebastian. *'This,'* she thought *'must be fate.'* She was face to face with her very own screen hero. Lily grew very fond of soldier Fred who would call each evening to take her home. The Sebastian film finished and she didn't feel half so sad now that Fred was around, but good things come to an end. Just as she was beginning to fall in love Fred had to return to barracks.

Lily was heartbroken as they said their farewells, Fred held her tightly and kissed her on quivering lips, promising faithfully to write as soon as he could. Her handkerchief was sodden as she tried to wave goodbye. The train pulled slowly out of the station until Fred was out of sight. Would she really see him again or was she just his date while on leave? She tormented herself with questions as she cried herself to sleep.

It was her turn to clean the picture house and even though a new Sebastian film was showing, the excitement wasn't quite the same; the manager had left early to bank the takings; the projectionist gone home, Sally and Lily were left in charge to round off the day. Sally, being the longer-serving, handled the keys, only the main door was left unlocked, the manager ensuring the others were secured before he left. Tonight, Sally felt unwell but needed the extra pennies and was determined to earn her pay. Lily offered to work alone just for one evening and wouldn't tell the manager that Sally had left early.

'You're a real pal, Lily,' said Sally between moans over her stomach pains. 'I'll do the same for you one day,' she declared, handing over the keys. All finished, she didn't realise the work of two people would take so much out of her. She sat on the front row and unwrapped a welcoming toffee, the taste of caramel and energy-giving sugar restored her; slowly her mind drifted over recent events. She wondered why Fred hadn't written yet or indeed if ever he would, then tossing her head before the tears could well, she muttered, 'Men!' The word echoed around the empty picture house back to those lonely ears. Gazing down she spied a discarded film magazine, retrieving it for the rubbish tip, she was intrigued by the headline. Talkies were on their way, she'd heard news of them and couldn't wait to see the first film.

'How wonderful to actually hear the actors speak,' she thought; suddenly she was wrenched back to reality, clearly she heard footsteps behind her. Turning, she hoped it would be the manager yet for Sally's sake hoped that it wasn't. There in the misty gloom a young man approached, she could just make out the uniform, it was *Fred!*

Lily called his name and leaping to her feet she ran towards his open arms, as he kissed her eager mouth his newly grown moustache tickled her lips.

'Hello Fred' she smiled broadly, he took her fingers, entwining them in his own.

'I've come to take you home.' he said. His voice was gruff and deep, she found it difficult to distinguish the words. His grip tightened around her fingers until she could stand the pain no longer.

'Fred, please don't squeeze so hard, you're hurting me.' As she begged to be released he pulled her roughly towards him, with elation brushed away she could now smell the alcohol mingled with a strong odour of tobacco; a loud rasping cough belched from those pungent lungs, Lily was repelled.

'Let go Fred!' Lily became agitated but he would not comply. Down towards the stage he dragged her, rough hands now circling her wrists - she was his prisoner.

Six steps rose up towards the stage, Lily felt the pain of every one as he hauled her body over them. Prostrate, Lily lay across the floor while his figure loomed, open-legged over her, hands on hips he stared at his hostage.

'I don't like you anymore.' she screamed.

'You loved me once,' he croaked, the words almost incoherent.

'You're different now,' Lily retorted.

'I'm just the same' came the reply, 'it's my world that's changed. I'm in your world now,' his voice rose in anger as he glared at her, 'but you are coming back with me. I was a hero once, and they all wanted me but now it's all changed and they don't want me anymore!'

He dragged her to her feet, they were so close to the screen that Lily thought it would be damaged yet he stepped even nearer, his image transposed onto the screen; there stood Sebastian in all his former glory, the hero back in his own domain.

'I ruled this world once' she heard his voice from the screen for the first time, 'no one will listen to me, my voice has let me down. Come with me Lily.' The rasping gruffness of his voice changed a once heroic figure into a mumbling villain.

His hand emerged from beyond the screen drawing Lily forward, she felt her body quake and stared at her arm, it seemed to quiver and like oil on water, flowed towards the screen. She couldn't pull back, he was too strong but she wasn't ready to ride into his sunset.

'I don't want your world,' she screamed. Then out of nowhere, Lily's free arm was grasped and an almighty tug freed her from her fate. Out she tumbled, headlong down the steps. There stood two highly-polished boots. Fred picked her, trembling, from the floor.

'Clumsy as ever,' he chuckled, 'sorry I didn't write,' he continued, 'I had an accident, I was in hospital for weeks.'

He spoke quietly pronouncing each word distinctly,

'Then I came to find you.'

As she kissed him, Lily noticed the wound on Fred's throat, only then did she realise, she held a real live hero in her arms. Her sunset was with Fred.

ADRIFT
Jane Ward

I woke suddenly. The train had jolted to a halt, depositing my handbag and most of its contents on the carriage floor. My mouth had the dryness of a long, deep sleep, and my eyes felt gritty and heavy-lidded. It seemed that I picked up my things with great slowness. Why did I feel so awful? My body and brain worked against each other. Where were we anyway? I didn't recognise anything. The grey, wet day was smudged by the beaded rain on the grimy windows. It had been such a beautiful morning when I left for work. I couldn't imagine how it had changed so quickly. Then, I felt the heat of shock rise from my stomach to my face. I was in a different seat, a different carriage from the one I had been in. This wasn't my usual local train. This was an Intercity Express. Looking round in disbelief I tried to think calmly and logically. I was good at that, so everyone told me. I remembered getting up as usual, having two cups of tea and two digestive biscuits, my usual breakfast, taking a cup to Michael and catching the 8.05 train for the forty minute journey to Lincoln. It was 11.20 by my watch. I stared at it.

A family row erupted at a table further down. Some people were reading, really reading, books and papers. Others were not reading, but turning pages of magazines carelessly, impatiently, trying to shorten their journey of boredom. At the table across the aisle a bright young thing kept dipping into a briefcase like a bird feeding. With his calculator and papers he exuded a confidence which exaggerated my present lack of it. I needed to fix myself to what I knew, and bring order out of the confusion in my mind. There had to be a logical explanation. I checked my handbag first. Everything seemed to be there: purse, keys, make-up, diary.

Diary! I turned rapidly to Friday 5th June.

Bellingham	-	*Divorce*	*10.00 am*
Fergus	-	*Will*	*11.30 am*
Juvenile Court	-		*2.00 pm*

I reached for my briefcase. It wasn't there . . . another shock! Nothing was real. I was adrift from reality, on a train I hadn't got on, briefcase stolen, more than three hours lost.

11.21 the train was gliding along smoothly once more, but where to? I quickly found my purse again and looked at the tickets there. *Grantham to Edinburgh, 12th June.* I closed my eyes - disorientated, already tired and impatient with the impossibility of it all. My mind worried the bone of doubt about what was wrong with me. I had lost my memory, but what had happened to me? A girl behind was crying, hiccuping incoherent words full of anguish while her companion made reassuring remarks. As he walked down the gangway, a middle-aged man folded up his paper and dropped it on a seat nearby. I grabbed it.

Above the huge headline, 'Train Disaster Caused By Bomb' was the date, neat and clear, 12th June 1990. Not a few hours lost then, but a whole week. I checked my diary again. All the appointments were neatly entered as I remembered but I had no memory of keeping any of them. What about my partners and my clients? What about Michael? That was the answer. To phone Michael from Edinburgh and find out what was going on. He would know.

I vaguely scanned the front page story of an explosion outside Edinburgh Station which had derailed a train into the path of another on the night of Wednesday 10th June. Eighty-five dead and over 100 injured. Pictures of distorted metal, like modern sculpture, showed carriages teetering above back gardens and others on their backs like science-fiction insets. It was the stuff of nightmares and I was lost, knowing nothing and apparently having no control. But soon I could phone Michael.

11.28 an announcement came thinly from the guard, his words vibrating within the metal like a fly in a tin. 'Owing to the crash, the train would terminate at Dunbar, and coaches would be waiting to complete the journey to Edinburgh'.

But where was I going and why? I checked the tickets again. One outward and one return. There must be a reason for everything. The thought of reaching a phone held me on solid ground amidst the quicksand of panic.

The train pulled into Dunbar at last, as the rain streamed down the windows in smooth diagonals from the roof. I got out behind the sobbing girl. A young man collected holdalls and anoraks. I had only my handbag. No mac or umbrella. It had been such a lovely day.

We all moved slowly out of the station. A row of coaches stood to attention, and several police and officials with transmitters and clip-boards came towards us. They regretted the inconvenience, but hoped the public would co-operate with the inquiry into the explosion. Information about victims could be obtained from the Incident Van etc. I looked for a phone but couldn't see one. As I moved towards a WPC to ask, the crying girl fainted in front of me, the rain wetting her blotchy face and smoothing her hair. As we lifted her up, the WPC the boy and me, I heard him saying that she had come because her parents were in the crash, and how awful it was not knowing for sure. It might not be them. They could be OK or just injured. We sat her down in the Incident Van while smelling salts and water were fetched. I watched detached as the dark stains of dirty wetness spread across her back. Wanting a phone seemed so insignificant beside the girl's mountain of grief, but I could hardly bear my impatience. A list on a blackboard headed 'For Identification' caught my attention, and at the bottom the name Sherrard (Michael Philip) held me. I heard a high-pitched whine in my ears and perspiration felt cold on my face. Now the nightmare really began as shock and fear fed my imagination within the sweating panic, as the adrenaline released the fluttering nausea and the deafening heartbeats, until noiseless cries were forced from my throat to end it.

'Where is the phone please?'
My voice was so far away I hardly heard it. The WPC asked me to sit down.
'Are you ill?' she repeated.
I couldn't explain this day to myself, let alone someone else. So I just asked again about a phone. I soon found it, then with trembling fingers got through to the school where Michael was headteacher.

'Can I speak to Mr Sherrard please?' I very nearly added 'It's his wife,' but I couldn't today.

'I'm very sorry, but Mr Sherrard is away on a Course and won't be in today'.

Michael never went away in term-time. I didn't recognise my voice as I said, 'In Edinburgh?'

She replied, 'Yes. Can I take a message?'

I put the phone down on the waiting silence, and felt my blouse damp and cold on my back.

I dragged my reluctant legs back to the van, and the rain anointed my sick fear at the inevitability of it all. 'I am Mrs Sherrard'. I told the WPC.

Her voice drifted round me.

'We can't be sure, of course. So many victims and so many personal effects, but in three coaches there were no survivors. We would be very grateful if you could see if your husband is among the dead. I'm so very sorry. We'll take you with the others. Are you alone? You shouldn't be alone at a time like this'.

I didn't understand about *times like this!*

On the mini-bus to the Royal Infirmary where all the victims had been taken, anger and resentment filled me. I resented the others on the bus who apparently understood all that had happened, and was furious with myself for being caught up in an impossible situation, but seated before a business-like desk all I felt was apprehension.

'Could you tell me about your husband, Mrs Sherrard?' The tired man sat, waiting to write. 'How old, how tall and so on, so that we can eliminate as many as possible. You understand?'

As I waited in the too-tidy office, footsteps and voices approached and receded up and down the hospital corridor in waves of busy rhythm. I carefully went over the events of the day, again and again, trying to bring reason to the unreasonable, sense to the nonsense. The man at last returned and let me through the usual maze of corridors to a cleared ward. 'Closure due to cuts, I'm afraid'. Neat rows of canvas bodies waited to be claimed, like lost luggage.

'We think your husband may be one of these victims, Mrs Sherrard. 'Tell me when you're ready'. I nodded but closed my eyes, then looked at the cold face. White and bruised, but not Michael. Then the next and the next. Only half a face but not Michael. But the next face . . .

distorted by livid cuts and bruises . . . I stared and felt the coldness that was his.

It slowly came from the floor. I was sinking into it. Disappearing. As the ice reached my head I screamed at the awfulness of everything and fell through space. My scream became the alarm. I sat up and held my head and felt the tension of fear drain through my fingers. It was 5.00 am. Rain drummed steadily against my quietening mind as reality returned. Then I saw that beside me the bed was smooth, empty, cold. Today was the 12th June.

LAY WORSHIP
Robert D Shooter

The silence of the still building welcomed him after the howling wind and dashing rain he had been enduring outside.

Peter had thought that he was totally lost from his intended walk. Till the stepping stones across the River Wharfe, with the water lapping them, making the passage exciting, and with the church nearby, relocated him.

As he went up to the church, expected it locked in this day and age of vandalism, he thought of his younger self trotting by his Vicar father to church. He felt strangely found somehow. Not just this church proving him not lost, but the connection with his spiritual roots. He smiled at his rebelliousness taking a back seat as reflections flood in.

Until safely inside the church he had not realised just how tired he was. Fighting faith he had pushed on past Parcival Hall, where he could have sought Christian accommodation as he remembered from his going with family days now long gone. Yet he also knew that at twenty miles walking in these conditions, with a heavy pack, he had already been at his normal limit of endurance. Somehow a bed and breakfast in Grassington had been his goal. 'I'll go and get lodgings as soon as I've rested a bit,' he told himself knowing that the village was only a mile away now and along tracks, not muddy fields or sunken paths.

He felt so rested, the phrase he tried not to repeat, 'the peace, which knows no understanding,' went through his mind almost against his will. He took off his rucksack, noticing just how sodden it was. He found a pile of what he assumed were old hassocks to put it on.

'This church must be medieval or older,' he said aloud but to himself, looking round. 'So many flocks of Christians must have worshipped, sung, praised, been baptised, married and been buried here.' Part of him, in spite of his claim of agnosticism, welcomed their spirit and prayers. Like loving arms stretching out to welcome him, his imagination told him. He knew part of his brain was still trying to resist the atmosphere that the church was bringing to him but compared with the evil wind outside he welcomed that conflict.

'A bit of theological bone to chew on,' as his Dad might have said. But he did not fight that thought, or remembrance of times past, but smiled in recognition.

'Poor disillusioned soul!' He thought fondly about his father, still a practising priest. 'Good Lord deliver us!' He shouted at the top of his voice, enjoying the echoes all round. He laughed maniacally but was not so happy with that.

Just then the lights went out. He went and put them back on. He took off his waterproofed outer garments putting them carefully over the altar rail to drip-dry. 'Living water!' he joked to himself and God, should there be a God and he was listening. He put his boots on the floor under the altar. He shivered. He could really do with a hot bath. He picked up his map, still in its waterproof cover, checking that he was very near to Grassington centre. He would find a nice Inn, have a good meal and a clean bed for the night. He had not been sleeping well in the rough, even though his tent was waterproof, as his imagination had kept him awake with strange unknown creatures prowling round outside ready to tear through the canvas. He laughed to himself. 'A hot bath; a good meal, here I come!' Yet his resolve faltered as he thought of the wind and the rain outside. He vowed just a few minutes to rest, and then he would go. Finding that underneath he was relatively dry, and that warm cassocks, or some dry material within reach made him feel warmer with it covering him, he fell asleep before the light went out again.

Peter had the best night's sleep he had had in years. He was in a dream. He was a treble again singing in this wonderful choir. 'Once in Royal David's City,' sang this lone strong treble. In his dream he checked whether it was he singing but it wasn't, 'stood a lowly cattle shed.' The lovely voice went on. In his mind he followed the words, 'where a Mother laid her baby in a manger for his bed. Mary was that mother mild, Jesus Christ her little child.'

It was at the start of the second verse, 'He came down to earth from Heaven,' that he became concerned for there was no tenor following their line. He could hear the harmony of the others but only the organ held the tenor line. That was terrible for it was such a lovely line. Then, in his dream, he told himself off. 'You daft twit,' he told himself severely, 'you are the one who should be holding that line!'

So he did. He lifted his magnificent tenor voice up in his sleep and his rich quality rang through the church equalling the other parts to give an harmonic whole. It was only when he felt uncomfortable singing in a lying position, that he shifted to do better justice to the sound. A truly lovely sound came out. Only to suddenly stop. When he stopped the choir carried on but without tenor.

Peter sat up amazed and frightened. 'Oh God!' He was in a fully lit church. It had a full congregation and the choir was almost at their seats. He alone had the altar area to himself.

'Maybe no-one has noticed me!' He thought hopefully, but noticing the grins and nudges on the part of the young boy and girl singers he knew that to be a forlorn hope.

He tried to stand up but the cassocks around him prevented that. It was perhaps as well for under the cassocks he just had his red underpants on. His trousers and socks, wet in part, were resting on the altar rail.

With sudden inspiration he put the Cassock properly on him, as it would be standing, not as a sheet or blanket, and stood up. He winked at the children smiling at him, and joined in at full voice. Again the only voice covering the wonderful tenor line, 'and He leads His children on to the place where He is gone.' He sat with the choir in the place where he assumed the tenors would sit if there were any. At this, the whole choir smiled at him as they sat down. He could not help himself. He beamed back. He realised that he felt at home. Unaccountably and unwillingly he realised that he was part of a Christmas Day service and it felt all right.

As the priest most carefully and reverently moved his drying garments from the altar rail to a handy chair nearby, he also felt that he must take communion. The first time in years but he was dying for breakfast. Bread and wine on the way could not but help, he told himself.

'At least there is no one here, who can tell my Dad,' he thought and then laughed at the ludicrousness of it all. He would have to tell his Dad this story himself!

THE WOMAN IN THE BLACK-EDGED VEIL
Nicola Grant

I moved into my new house at the edge of the village on a chilly, frosty morning. I had just secured my first teaching post in a town seven miles away. The house was perfect. It was in easy travelling distance for work and yet it was spacious and had a rural charm. The nearest building to the house was an old church. In fact the house had once been the vicarage. The church was derelict. Its stained glass missed fragments; the guttering was coming away from the masonry. The churchyard, with its slanting gravestones, was overgrown. The grass had not been mown for years and the hedgerow was untamed.

This was my new home and I had plans for it. I had the usual problems associated with any move. My teapot had lost its spout due to careless packing and I realised the curtains I had thought would suffice for the front room would be several inches too short. By the time I had brought some semblance of order to the house it was already twilight. I made myself a light supper, I was beginning to feel faint having not eaten all day, then settled myself in my favourite armchair with a good book. After an hour or so my eyelids began to droop and I yawningly went to bed.

The first night in a strange room is always filled with odd noises and unfamiliar shadows. The glass rattled against the window frame. Animals cried in the distance; hunting or being hunted. Sleep was eluding me and then came the light. A circle of bright light against the window, like someone was holding a candle against the pane. I sat bolt upright in my bed and reached for my dressing gown. It must have been some juvenile prank. The light seemed to recede towards the church and I decided to investigate.

It was cold in my garden and in the churchyard. The tall, wet grass slapped at my feet as I ran following the light. I had no torch having left the house in haste and I soon realised my error. Something lay in my path hidden by the grass. My foot struck it and I pitched forward unable to stop myself from falling. There I lay until dawn broke and I regained consciousness. My foot was swollen, my head bruised, but at least no bones were broken. I had tripped over the broken top of a gravestone. It read 'Anna Pargeter d.1817'. There was no mention of her relation to another. She was not the 'dearly departed', 'wife of', 'daughter of' or 'sadly missed'. Her death was stated as a clinical fact, cold and brutal. Struggling to my feet I was determined to learn all about Anna Pargeter.

The doctor came to bandage my foot and enquired how I had injured it. I felt foolish saying I had been roaming around the churchyard at midnight following a phantom light. The doctor said I obviously had not heard the rumours of the ghost of Anna. I must have paled visibly as he assured me it was just local folklore with no substance. I said I wanted to know what the tale was. This is what he told me . . .

Anna was a young woman of good family who had money but no title. Her family arranged a marriage telling her that if she did not go along with it she would be cut-off and left penniless. Without any real choice, Anna married Mr Pargeter. His family were respected in the county but they had lost their wealth due to a series of bad investments. Soon after the marriage Anna complained of feeling unwell, of pains in the stomach. She said Mr Pargeter had only married her for her money and was trying to murder her. Her family refused to believe her, saying it was a ruse to get the marriage annulled. Anna persisted in her view and said that when her husband killed her she would haunt the church and its grounds until he was brought to justice.

Anna died and was buried in the churchyard. Her family still treated Mr Pargeter as a son. He never visited Anna's grave and within a week a young girl from the village was seen walking publicly with him. He bought her expensive clothes, perfume and jewellery. Within two weeks he had announced his intention to marry her. Still no one believed that Anna had been murdered.

The church reputedly became haunted by her. What is known is that a series of vicars refused to work there and others became mad saying they had seen the woman with the candle and the black-edged veil.

The doctor assured me it was just superstition. I knew what I had seen and decided to do some research. The facts seemed to support Anna's assertion; her husband had murdered her.

Anna had died from arsenic poisoning, accidental it was said. She was only twenty-six years old. Two months after her death, Mr Pargeter married Martha Baker and within two years Martha died of arsenic poisoning. Mr Pargeter was sentenced to death for the murder of Martha but no further investigation was carried out regarding Anna's demise. Mr Pargeter was hanged at Reading gaol in 1820 still protesting his innocence.

Then the light came again. A round circle against the windowpane which receded into the churchyard. I followed through the churchyard and into the church. This time I had a small torch and I negotiated the crumbling gravestones without injury. I entered the church. There she stood by the altar. A long black dress hid her body and a black-edged veil shrouded her face. In her hand she carried a candle. This was no living woman but the apparition of a troubled spirit. I was transfixed unable to come closer to her but I knew what I had to tell her.

'Anna, I believe you,' I began 'I know he poisoned you but he is dead now. Anna, please be at peace.'

It was as if I had muttered some magic incantation. The apparition retreated along the transept. I backed away and went home.

There have been no more sightings of Anna. I have had her gravestone restored and every Sunday I place flowers there. Rest in peace Anna.

ECHO
Jackie Bilton

The day Hannah sat me down - I cried.

She asked me to look at her jewellery and choose what I wanted. It shone in different colours. When I was a child I had lovingly watched her wear it to finish off an outfit. I'd believed I'd seen a million sparkling diamonds. I remember I'd secretly pin brooches on my nightie when I'd been sent to bed early and puff my face with her power. She loved her jewellery and so did I.

I'd listen to her music box and watch the ballerina that danced on top, dreaming that it would be me some day. But in a heartbeat I was older and she was dying. She had asked me to choose what I wanted. What could I say to her? 'Don't hurt me?' But on reflection, who was hurting? I cried, and for the first time in my life she couldn't console me. She told me to pull myself together and I didn't want to; she kept control, stone-faced, hoping that I'd accept something. She needed it to go where it would be loved and she would be remembered. I knew I had to be strong for her, it was what she was asking me to be. I couldn't say 'Hold me!' Over and over again I said 'Nan you'll need these next year.'

I chose one small mauve brooch studded with stones and as I held it I realised it was only made of paste. I stared in the mirror and caught her reflection as she searched through things she'd lovingly kept for over fifty years. Something Diana had given her, or us girls. Everything faded and a little torn, but still giving pleasure.

Her small body was hunched and emaciated, her eyes slightly glazed. I'd wondered for a while if she'd run through corn as a child. She'd arrived in the time of horse-drawn carriages and parlour maids. Of living in shadowed back streets and bathing in tin baths. Her beautiful fingers had touched roses, cradled babies and helped mend broken hearts. Dan her husband had died thirteen years before. She'd born her loneliness with dignity, having told me she'd talked to him every night in the clouds, quite convincing me that he'd talked back. She was not now the fine figure of a woman I'd watched over forty years before. But still held her head with pride. I'd looked at her jewellery for the last time, and breaking, walked away, I hadn't the heart to tell her I wanted it all.

Diana, Hannah's daughter consoled me. She reminded me of my teenage years saying 'I had hopes for you.'

We looked at photographs of us both twenty years before, so much firmer, we both had fire. But now, like Hannah, the years were creeping up on us, wearing away our tight skins and young hearts. Today I think of the times Diana tilted me into the wind with her hand not far behind me, ready to catch me when I fell. Of the heartache and joys of growing up and being afraid. New freedoms and yet always the need to run back to the nest. As a teenager always going against everything she'd advised, hearing, 'Don't forget to ring!' as I flew out through the door.

Now we sit quietly and remember. She shares her secrets and as always I love to listen.

I reach in my drawer and pick out one small mauve brooch and pass it to a beautiful blonde young woman who sits next to me. Her confidence shining, eyes piercing blue, one with much fire. One with a need to go against everything I say. 'The one I have hopes for!' I always hear myself saying 'For God's sake, drive carefully.'

I pass the brooch to her saying 'Look after this, it's only paste, but like you . . . it's a jewel in my heart.'

SOME BECOME BEAUTIFUL
Linda Jefferies

'Some Become Beautiful' was at last beginning to make a profit. Jenny had worked so hard to make her life's dream a reality. The salon was tastefully decorated in muted shades of yellow and furnished with wicker seating covered with primrose scatter cushions. The whole ensemble creating a relaxed atmosphere, which would cocoon all whom entered the shop. A Clairol advert featuring Kate Moss gazed down on Jenny and the customer she attended. Hairspray and soapy scents clung to the air; this was Jenny's world. Jenny was a quiet girl who radiated happiness, had done since a child. Smiling, she handed the elderly customer her change. The lady beamed back thanking her. Jenny picked up her pen and scanned the appointment book. 'Same time next week Mrs Jones?'

'Yes please dear' she nodded, 'a rinse and set.' Jenny jotted it down. 'OK we'll see you then, bye.'
Mrs Jones waved as she closed the door; chimes rang out till it clicked shut. Jenny glanced at the next appointment, her heart almost stopped when she caught sight of the name. Panic rose in her throat, her head shot up, 'Yvonne, there's a Mrs Coldstone due to me at two. It's not the teacher from the Comprehensive up the road is it?'
Yvonne rolled her eyes. 'Yes unfortunately, I take it you know her well, judging by your expression.' Jenny nodded, swallowing convulsively,. 'She . . . she took a dislike to me at school, almost bordering on hate.'
'How could anyone hate you?'
'She did. She made my life a misery. Mrs Coldstone could be very cruel when she chose to, revelling in the humiliation of those she disliked.'
Shuddering with revulsion, Jenny covered her face with her hands.
Yvonne shook her head and sighed, 'Yes I can believe it, I've met her once or twice. Do you want me to do her? You can have Mrs Thomas!'
Jenny combed her fingers through her dark silky hair, 'No! I must conquer my fear, I'll do it.'
Yvonne glanced out of the window, reaching out to squeeze Jenny's hand. 'Here comes the old battleaxe now, keep smiling Jen.'

As if sensing danger, the bell jangled wildly as the door flung open. A stout, tall woman strode in, beady blue eyes bore into the two women standing behind the counter. Looking down her nose, she surveyed them disdainfully, thin lips compressed, magnifying her meanness, her mouth almost disappearing into her face. Jenny's thoughts ran riot. 'I will not be afraid of her. I'm not a child she cannot intimidate me now.'

Jenny mustered up every scrap of confidence she had and smiled 'Good afternoon Mrs Coldstone, if you'll just take a seat, I'll be with you in a moment.'

The bell on the door tinkled as Mrs Thomas walked in. Mrs Coldstone glared at Jenny, 'Do you have to do my hair, I want an experienced stylist?' Her bellow rang through the shop.
Mrs Thomas jumped as she hung up her coat. Jenny stepped back, took a deep breath looked her in the eyes and said. 'I am a professional stylist with ten years experience.' She waved standing to her full height of 5ft her hand artistically towards certificates decorating the wall. Mrs Coldstone's eyes turned to slits; she gave an exaggerated sigh and turned her back on Jenny. Mrs Thomas tutted and shook her head. Mrs Coldstone glared, withering her with one glance.

Later as Jenny washed Mrs Coldstone's hair, her thoughts wandered again. Unhappy memories surfaced, memories that were buried long ago. Joyful images of drowning the hateful woman swam around in her head. Slowly the bellowing of a cow in deep distress filtered through her hazy thoughts. 'Are you trying to drown me *girl*?' Her voice getting louder by the second. *I wish I could!* Jenny thought as her trembling hands wrapped the towel around her head. Desperately wanting to smother her, Jenny rubbed her hair roughly. *Why tag on the word - girl?* It really rankled Jenny. *I do have a name!* 'Not so hard *girl*!' The complaints fast flowing like rainwater along a gutter. Jenny smiled thinly, 'Sorry Mrs Coldstone, but we don't want water everywhere do we? Someone might slip.' Jenny's voice dripped with sarcasm. She led the woman to the chair. As she snipped away, revenge quivered on the tip of her scissors but guilt and common sense won through. *Why sink to her level, show her how good you are!*

For two hours Jenny weaved miracle upon miracle as she permed Mrs Coldstone's hair, making her look almost human. Staring haughtily in the mirror she began to preen herself. 'Not bad, you've progressed I'll agree but there's always room for improvement.' Her eyes lanced through Jenny, willing her to disagree. Jenny gave a cool smile while gritting her teeth and firmly stated, 'Well Mrs Coldstone, you should know.' Slowly she walked to the counter and made out the receipt. 'What do you mean *girl?*' Mrs Coldstone demanded as she slapped the money down on the counter. 'Well you're certainly not perfect. The way you treat people proves that and another thing, my name isn't *girl*, it's Jenny. *J E N N Y,* it always has been. I'm a grown woman running my own business, so please show some respect.' Mrs Coldstone stoodopen-mouthed like a fish on a monger's slab. Paying quickly, she shrugged into her coat and made to leave. 'I'll not bring my custom here again, I like to be treated with respect due to my years.' The door slammed and she was gone.

Looking at Yvonne in surprise Jenny murmured, 'So do I!' Sagging after the anticlimax of her ordeal, Jenny sniffed, 'Our job is to make people beautiful but she had no chance.' Mrs Thomas agreed wholeheartedly. 'Yes dear, it's a head transplant she needs, her hair looked fine.' Yvonne doubled up with laughter, tears coursing down her cheeks. Hugging Jenny close, she smiled, 'You make me so proud *girl.'* Shaking her head with disbelief at finding she'd finally won, Jenny wiggled a dance of victory and giggled, 'Anyone for coffee?'

BUSINESS MINDED
Dan Sampson

Viceroy and Barber lay in bed. It was a clear, silent night and the summer breeze sauntered in through the half-open window opposite the foot of the bed, causing the light linen sheets to rise, and then gently fall again.

'Can't be done,' said Viceroy. 'Impossible.'

'Probably.' replied Barber. 'But wouldn't it be great. Whoever could turn that one over would be set for life. Millions, hundreds of millions.'

'There's security like Fort Knox.'

'Right! And just about as much money.'

Viceroy and Barber had been workmates at a factory, bottling Gin and other spirits. Both laid off, they had tried other jobs but soon gave up; postman, bartender, ticket collector, usher. Regular jobs were just not for them, so they had become friends, then lovers, and then stick-up kids.

Barber was short about 5' 2'' with long brown hair, her eyes as black as an eight ball, and she had a powerful air about her. Viceroy was not much bigger than she was, about 5' 9'' but broad across the shoulders and had a hard, harsh face, embittered by years of bureaucratic injustices. He called himself *disenfranchised!*

'There are millions of us, you know.' He would say to Barber. 'Millions of *disenfranchised* workers.' Barber would just nod her head, trying to disguise her indifference.

They were talking about the First Community bank, in the town of Mantion, about eight miles up the road from the motel they were staying in. It held all of the peoples' money that lived in the town, as it was the only bank for about fifty miles. There were probably three or four hundred thousand people in Mantion, and this bank held all of their money. All of it. But, with the exclusive bank came its unrivalled security, and this was always a problem.

Barber said it probably could be done. Viceroy said it couldn't. Not with just two of them.

Being partners in crime brought with it a level of paranoia that does not accompany any other type of partnership. And this always bothered Barber. If nobody else could trust Viceroy, then why should she feel like she could? Viceroy felt the same way. Trust does not come easy amongst thieves. Honour? Out of the question.

At breakfast, Viceroy sat in silence at the scratched and marked wooden table, his eyes fixed on the newspaper, concentrating so hard he could have burnt a hole through it. Finally, he murmured something about meeting an old friend that day and he would not be home until early the next morning and that there was nothing to worry about but he just thought he better tell her so she would not be worried. All the while his eyes stayed firmly on the paper in front of him.

Barber sensed that there was something wrong, but still she did not question him. Viceroy got up from the table and put on his black patrol jacket. He patted his pockets softly to check for his keys and wallet, leant forward and kissed Barber on the cheek and made his way to the door.
'See ya, honey' he said over his shoulder, smiling.
'Soon, I hope.' she replied, in a cool monotone, that belied her restless suspicion.
Barber did not take her eyes off him. Viceroy walked out of the door and closed it gently behind him.
She sat and stared out of the window into the sunlight, wondering where he was going. The day was long and hot, and Viceroy's whereabouts were still on her mind. She did not care what he was doing, as long as he came back at the end of the day. Well, she cared about some things he could do, but being with another woman was not one of them. All men lie, especially Viceroy. What really concerned her was that he would make enough money to leave her behind and disappear forever. Not because she wanted to be with him, she just wanted to be the one to do the leaving. After several hours of turning it over in her mind she went out to meet her associates. She had some business to attend to, too.

She did not wake when Viceroy finally returned, and at breakfast she saw the morning newspaper and smiled.
'Told you it could be done.' she said proudly, and dropped the paper in front of him, the headline read; *First Community Bank Held Up. Hundreds Of Millions Taken.*
Viceroy just shrugged his shoulders, evidently unimpressed.
'Aren't you surprised?' she asked, looking over his shoulder.

'I guess so.' came the reply.

Barber noticed that Viceroy would not look at her, and this troubled her. 'What's going on with you?' she asked. 'You know something about this?'

'No!' he replied. 'You?'

'No!'

'Then why are you looking so proud then?' he quizzed, turning in his chair to look at her.

'No reason, I mean, I'm not . . . ' she stammered, backing away, wary of Viceroy's temper. 'You know something about this, do you?' he shouted.

'Not at all.' she shouted back.

A tense silence fell on the pair of them. Viceroy turned back to the table and continued eating. The day was hotter and closer than before, made even more so by the atmosphere between them. She was suspicious of him, and him of her.

At last she broke.

'Where were you last night? she asked.

Viceroy looked up. 'Out!'

'Where?'

'Somewhere. With friends.'

'You turned over that bank, didn't you? You turned it over and then you were going to disappear. You only came back today to pick up your stuff.'

'You're insane, Barber, you are insane. And as a matter of fact I think you cracked that bank and are just accusing me of it so you can get really mad and walk out on me and never come back, which then means you're free.'

'No way!' She shook her head. 'You're paranoid.'

'Yes way. I don't know where you were yesterday, do I? You could have been anywhere with anyone, doing anything?'

'Well I wasn't. And anyway I could say the same about you.'

'Is that a fact?'

'Yes!' she replied and silence fell in on them again. After a few minutes, as if cued to do so, they both broke the silence.

'Where's the money? they said together.

Viceroy and Barber stared at each other, speechless. Viceroy got up from his seat at the table and said 'I'm going out for a long time and when I get back we're going to sort this out.'

'You walk out of that door, and I'll never see you again, what do you think I am stupid or something?' she shouted.

'Paranoid!' he shouted back.

'Where's the money, you snake?' She growled, through gritted teeth.

'Insane!' said Viceroy shaking his head and tapping a finger on his temple. He moved towards the door, and Barber sprang at the table and pulled out a chrome-plated pistol from her bag that was resting on top of it. She pointed it at Viceroy and locked the trigger. Hearing the menacing 'click', Viceroy stopped and turned around, slowly.

'You go and you're dead!'

'You're mad. Mad!'

'No! Just *business-minded.*' she said and shot him three times in the chest. Barber turned and picked up her bag, and put the pistol back into it. She then hurried into the bedroom and pulled three sports bags full of untraceable, non-sequential bills from under the bed. Her share of the First Community Bank raid.

She half ran out of the door and met her accomplices, or as Barber would put it, her associates, who were waiting in the car park.

Barber had been part of that raid. Viceroy's going away for the night had given her a twelve or fourteen hour window to do the robbery and get back home before he did. And of course she could not just disappear because there was a chance that he might find her. Somehow. One thing did surprise her though, she did not think that he would work her out so quickly, she did not think he would see through her plan.

Nonetheless, she had to be sure that he would not find her, and killing him was the only way, after all - he would have probably killed her.

Business-minded, you see.

GOING OUR SEPARATE WAYS
Kimberly Harries

They had one more day together, until they both went their separate ways. Marisa planned to spend every minute with her brother, Charlie. She had the whole day set out perfectly. In the morning they would make a massive breakfast together, with pancakes and waffles. For lunch they would go for a walk and talk about old times. Then in the evening she would spring her surprise party, which she was sure he already knew about. She had already invited his friends and hers. It would be the perfect day. Marisa smiled at her reflection in the mirror. She turned off her light and jumped into her bed. She hoped Charlie had a good life in Cardiff. He was going to Cardiff University, where he would study physiotherapy. She was going to miss him. She could tell him anything, they were really close. She closed her eyes and tried with all her might to sleep but sleep eluded her.

In the morning, she looked at her tired reflection in the mirror. Her eyes were red from lack of sleep. She put some make-up on, which made her look ten times better. She hoped Charlie wasn't up yet. She wanted to surprise him with the breakfast. She pulled on a pale blue dress and brushed her long blonde hair. Charlie was eighteen and she was sixteen. Two weeks ago she had got her GCSE results. She had passed with flying colours. She hadn't got anything below a C. Her brother had done better two years ago.

Physiotherapy had been Charlie's second choice, he hadn't got into his first choice of a career. Originally he had wanted to be a geologist. Marisa didn't know what she wanted to do with her life. She liked writing stories, but knew that it was near to impossible for her to do that as a career. She went downstairs into the kitchen. Marisa's mouth hung open. Her parents and Charlie were sitting at the kitchen table. The table was covered with food. Charlie was putting syrup onto his pancakes. She clenched her fists. She had told her parents the day before that she was going to make the breakfast. She felt like crying, they had ruined everything. Charlie patted the seat next to him and she reluctantly sat down.

'I'm sorry but your father got so hungry. You know what he's like first thing in the morning,' her mother laughed.

'Come on Dot, give me a break,' her father joined in the joke.

Marisa rolled her eyes and Charlie winked at her.

'I was just telling the truth, Keith.'

They kissed and hugged each other. She grabbed a pancake and ate it quickly. She always got embarrassed when her parents kissed right in front of her. She knew that she should be happy for them. Most couples after twenty years of marriage couldn't stand the sight of each other. At least they were still in love. She hoped that when she was twenty years into her marriage, she would still be in love with her husband. They pulled away but kept their hands entwined.

Marisa scooped a spoonful of syrup onto her second pancake and Charlie frowned. 'What?' she snapped a little to harshly. She quickly regretted the words.

He mother changed the subject. 'So Charlie what have you got planned for today?'

Marisa was just about to answer when her brother spoke. 'My friend got the day off work, we're going to play snooker together,' he smiled.

She would have told him to cancel it but he looked so happy. She sighed and looked at her plate. She still had the party to look forward to. Something will probably happen to ruin that as well. Charlie kissed her on the cheek and left.

'I'm sorry, I knew you wanted to spend the day with him' her mother sighed.

'Marisa's still got the party to look forward to, stop worrying Dot.'

She excused herself and went up to her parents' bedroom. She picked up the phone and called her best friend, Olivia and told her her plan. She wasn't going to sit around and wait for her brother to come home. She was going to accidentally bump into her brother and his friend. They always went to the same place to play snooker. Olivia arrived ten minutes later. She changed into a skirt and a blue top. They smiled at each other and left.

'Are you sure they're going to be there?'

'Of course they are, Olivia.'

They hurried their pace and went into the bowling place. They walked down the isle until they came to the snooker tables. Two were occupied and one was empty. Her brother was nowhere to be seen. Olivia shrugged her shoulders 'What now?'

'Maybe they got held up. We'll play a few games until they come.'
Marisa got the snooker cues and Olivia set up the balls. Marisa always won. When she was seven, Charlie had taken her there and had taught her how to play. They went nearly every week. She was nearly as good as him. Charlie had had two years more to learn. They played three games and she won all of them. She was beginning to get restless. Where were they? She couldn't control her impatience any longer. She went over to one of the pay phones and dialled Charlie's friend's number. Charlie answered on the forth ring. 'Hello?'
'Charlie, it's me, Marisa. I thought you were going to play snooker?' she asked accusingly.
'We were but Nick's mum came down with a stomach bug. So I suggested that we stayed. Anyway, it's fun, we're talking about old times. I've got to go, I'll see you at the party tonight.'
'You know about the party? It was supposed to be a surprise.'
'Mum told me.'
'Typical.'
'It doesn't matter, I knew anyway. I always know what you're thinking. I think it's a great idea. I'll see you then.'
Marisa hung up the phone. She forced herself not to cry. Everything was turning into a disaster. She hadn't spent more than a few minutes with him all day. She walked back over to Olivia and rolled her eyes. She didn't want her friend to see that she was upset. They played a few more games and left. They walked around for a while and talked. Charlie had been a good friend to Olivia. She was also going to miss him.

How was she going to cope without him around? Who was she going to talk to? Olivia wasn't around twenty-four hours a day. She could talk to her parents but they didn't understand the way her brother did.

They both went to her house, to set up the party. Her parents had already started to make the food. She would be busy doing the decorations. She already had bought him a leaving card. She also had a present for him. It was a really expensive watch. Olivia and Marisa pinned four balloons to the front door. They put a banner across the wall in the living room. It said 'Good Luck'. She set out the table with knives and forks. There would be a buffet in the corner of the room. She went up to her bedroom to look for some decent music.

Everything was set. The four of them sat down in the living room. They were all tired. Marisa's parents were smiling at each other. She could see the sadness in their eyes. They were really going to miss him. Although he had been a pain at times he had been their son and her brother. They would always love him. She would miss him but she would also envy him. He was starting his own life and making new friends. In two years' time she would be doing exactly the same thing. That was if she passed her 'A' levels. Her parents would be alone then.

'What time did he say he was coming?' her father asked.

'I don't know.'

'What do you mean, you don't know? Everybody's coming in fifteen minutes. If he's not here -'

'Keith, leave her alone. She just said she doesn't know. Charlie will be here and it's going to be the perfect evening.' She smiled at her husband.

'I hope so.'

The doorbell went and Marisa answered it. Two of Charlie's friends had arrived. She didn't know much about them. She hadn't really spoken to them. Olivia had invited them. They asked where Charlie was and she didn't know what to say. She picked up the phone to call his friend's house but nobody answered. They were probably on their way here. Why didn't the mother answer the phone? Wasn't she supposed to be sick? What if Charlie had lied to her? Maybe he was going somewhere with his friend. Surely he would have told her of his plans. No, he wouldn't lie to her, he was probably on his way over here right now.

She sat down next to Olivia. Her parents were talking to the two boys. They seemed to know more about them than she did. Marisa didn't join in the conversation. Her eyes were glued to the clock on the wall. As the seconds ticked by anxiety settled over her. More guests arrived and the party was under way. People were dancing and having fun. Nobody seemed to mind that the host of the party was not there. Nobody that was except for her. She couldn't enjoy herself knowing that Charlie wasn't there.

She had done all this for him and he hadn't turned up. She was angry with him. He had known about the party and he had promised to come. She wanted to cry, the whole day had been ruined. She wasn't going to see her brother for a whole month. He would come down for the weekend and then he would be gone again. All she had wanted to do was to spend one last day with him, before he left. She hadn't been asking for much even her parents were dancing. She couldn't shake the gloom that had settled over her. One of the boys came and sat down next to her. 'I'm Adam, you're Marisa, right?'

As if he didn't know? She didn't say that though. She tried to smile at him but failed. She nodded and looked at the floor.

'Charlie was a good friend. He always knew how to make me laugh, I'm gonna miss him,' he smiled.

This is more like a wake than a party. Everybody was talking as if Charlie was dead. The thought made her burst out laughing. Maybe her brother wasn't there but that didn't stop her from having fun. It wasn't as if she was never going to see him again. Charlie wasn't going that far away. She could always write to him. She would talk to him on the phone nearly every day. Adam smiled at her. She tried to control her laughter but failed. He was looking at her strangely. Finally she could speak. 'I'm sorry. I just thought of something that was really funny.'

'Would you like to dance?'

She smiled for the first time that night. 'Sure.'

She let him take her hand. They danced together. Olivia winked at her and she smiled. The rest of the night was fun.

After most of the people had left they all sat down and talked. Adam stayed behind with his friend. Olivia stayed. She found out more about him. The party had almost been a success, almost. It didn't matter how hard she tried to have fun, she couldn't. She was worried about Charlie. He had promised to be there, so where was he? Had something happened to him? She said goodbye to Adam and Olivia and sat down with her parents.

Her mother sighed. 'What a night! I'm shattered.'

'You go to bed and I'll clean up the mess,' Marisa suggested.

Her father shook his head. 'No, we'll all clean it up in the morning. Go to bed and stop worrying about Charlie, I'm sure he's fine.'

She smiled and went upstairs. She collapsed onto her bed and fell asleep. She had a nightmare about losing Charlie. It wasn't the nightmare that woke her, it was Charlie's voice. She opened her eyes and gasped.

He laughed down at her. 'Sorry I woke you.'

Marisa was happy to see that he was safe but she was also angry. 'Where were you?'

'I'm sorry. Nick's mum offered to drive us. You'll never guess what happened, we had two flat tyres. Nobody stopped to help us. We had to walk to the nearest pay phone and call a tow truck. I called home but nobody answered.'

'I've had the worst day.'

'I'm sorry. I know you wanted us to spend the day together. I wanted to be at the party and say goodbye to everybody, I really did. When I come down in one month we'll spend the day together, I promise. I'm going to miss you.'

'I'll miss you too. You're going to have a great time there.'

'We'll talk every day on the phone.'

'You promise?'

'I promise.'

'I love you. Go back to sleep.'

Charlie went to the door and smiled back at her. 'I love you too.'

The next day was the hardest day of her life. She had to say goodbye to her brother. They stood at the train station. Her mother was crying softly to herself. Her father gave him a big hug. 'We'll miss you. Phone us when you get there.'

Charlie nodded mutely. He hugged their mother and turned to her. They smiled at each other and hugged. She kissed him on the cheek. 'Bye my brother.'

'Bye my sister.'

He turned around and stepped onto the train. She watched as the train left the station and she smiled to herself. He would be all right and so would she.

B B AND E M
D G Brown

We stood outside the travel agents, I knew this was probably my last chance to change Mary's mind. I didn't fancy going abroad again as the last time I went all those foreigners kept trying to kill me, still after half a century they should have quietened down a bit. It was different in Mary, my beloved wife's case, she'd been to Filey and Yarmouth, but not real abroad.

'Now you're sure this is what you want, it's your endowment money?' Mary asked.

She was good at giving options with no choices. If I had been honest I would sooner have gone to Aintree to see the Grand National, going away for a fortnight wasn't even in my top ten, mentally I tossed a coin, heads for Mary, tails for Mary, I just nodded in agreement.

'Right, when I tip you the wink, you just sign the cheque, sometimes you can be a little darling, not often, but sometimes.'

This reminded me of the sweet young girl I'd married, and wondered what had happened to her, maybe she had lost herself trying to find me.

'You deserve only the best, I can't wait to take you away from all this, by courtesy of,' I looked at the sign over the shop door. 'Tarquin Entwhistle, established since 1997.'

All this sounded so romantic I had the urge, which I controlled, to sweep Mary up and carry her into the shop, as I couldn't risk doing my back in so near to my holidays.

We stood perusing the window, the magical sounding names, Spain, Morocco, Egypt, Aintree, was this a sign from above, I thought, looking at the spotty-faced youth behind the counter. If he was truly a messenger from on high, God was indeed scraping the barrel.

'Let me do all the talking,' Mary said, so no change there.

As the newly appointed doorman, I stood to one side, allowing Mary to make a beeline for the unsuspecting Spotty.

She banged her handbag down on the counter, causing Spot to jump, when he came down she gave him both barrels. 'Are you the person in charge?' she asked.

The lad answered in a tried and polite manner, just in case she was somebody from head office. 'It says in the small print we don't give refunds.'

'Then, it's just as well we haven't paid you any money, now, listen carefully, we want a nice quiet, cheap, sunny holiday, no bingo, no bookies, and most important, within walking distance of an all-night chemist.'

Her three years, as a corporal in Land Army, ordering people about, had stood her in good stead, plus all the practise she'd had on me. The lad, who even at his tender age, could see he was in for a battle, took two tablets and a sip of water. 'Are you sure you're not a spy from head office sent to wind me up?' he asked, convinced, like many of us, that Mary was not for real.

'Do I look like James Bond?' Mary stood there, daring him to be truthful.

The lad looked her up and down, then stood to one side, to do the same from a different angle. Now, I could understand how, in the half light, he could have been confused, but he decided to give her the benefit of the doubt. 'It's nice to see a customer who knows what you both want,' Spotty said, looking sympathetically at me, trying to draw me into the conversation.

I, being older and wiser was busy counting the squares in the carpet.

'Let me see what we can find,' he began thumbing his way through a pile of leaflets, 'You can call me Clive, all my friends do, did you come in answer to our advert in the paper?'

'No, we saw your card in the Post Office window, and you can call me Mrs Hacksley,' Mary replied, determined not to get too familiar with the staff.

If Clive only knew how lucky he was, we had been married four years before she let me call her Mary.

'Here we are,' said Clive, pulling out a large brochure, 'Ratvainia,' he quoted from the Travel Agents Bible, 'A small principality, hidden away between Nepal, and Outer Mongolia, I can show you on the map, it's just to the left of the V in Everest.'

'Everest, we're looking for somewhere a bit warmer than that,' said Mary hoping to nip young Clive in the bud, but he hadn't got his City and Guild in selling for nothing, ignoring his victim's plea, he pressed on.

'You don't want all that sun, carrying all that suntan lotion, restless nights with a sunburnt back, sweaty armpits, topless beaches.'

The thought of topless aroused my dormant animal instincts, but the idea of Mary topless quickly dampened them.

Now Clive had noticed the flicker of interest in my eyes and continued his attack. 'In Ratvainia, you'd have none of these worries, a balaclava, some thick socks, two or three pullovers, a spare ice pick, and you're on your way. Do you like sports Sir?' he asked.

I had been miles away, wondering how many hours of fun my grandchildren would have, joining his spots up with a biro. 'I don't mind the odd game of darts now and again,' said I, not used to having my opinion asked for.

'Then you'll love these people, they're all sports mad,' young Clive was up and running, 'Only last year a lady, from Atkin Street just round the corner, won their national ski jumping title, of course we never found out who pushed her, but not bad for a seventy-two year old. They treated her like a queen, some competitors said they would crown her if she came back to defend her title, and she would have, if we could have got her wheelchair up the gangway. I've got a snap of her somewhere.' Clive took a photo out of his wallet, 'That's her, peeping between the Lucozade and the Get Well card.'

Although fascinated Mary was not yet completely sold on the idea. 'It can't be very big, I've never heard of it,' she said, a subject she could speak on with some authority, as she had once scored fifty-seven in a geography test.

'That's mainly their own fault,' answered Clive, he read from the good book. 'In the year of thirteen twenty-two, when a high priest was translating their ancient hieroglyphic, he mistakenly misread circumcision for castration, if it wasn't for the fact that most of them were atheists they'd have died out years ago.'

Having decided this repartee had gone on long enough Mary started buttoning up her coat. 'We'll try somewhere else, somewhere the assistants have started shaving, we're more for old churches, museums, that sort of thing.'

'Culture,' said Clive, looking at me, who was busy finishing off his crossword. 'This place is teeming with it,' he read on, from his bible.

'In the main square in the capital Panisto, not fifty yards from your hotel, is the Great Well of Kardos, where in sixteen forty the Great Plague started. These waters are still being used today, mainly as a cure-all spa. Each Saturday night during the tourist season, (December to November) all are invited to the treading of the snow grapes in the square, where the town band plays music to stomp your feet too. In the interest of hygiene, any visitor suffering with verrucas or athletes foot are asked to keep their socks on. All tourists are warned to leave early, as the band's last number is the Ratvainian National Anthem, which sounds like The Flight Of The Bumblebee, and there's grape juice flying about all over.'

Clive wasn't going to be beaten by an old lady, and her nearly mute companion. Resorting to the travel agent's last gimmick, bribery, Clive continued. 'Tell you what I'll do, out of my own pocket, this real imitation leather Ratvainian cookery book, oxen and chips with ice, Yakburgher on toast with ice, boiled Panda's eggs with or without ice.' He then made the fatal mistake, which I had done many times, of pausing for breath, allowing Mary to jump in. 'No thank you, if that's the best you've got, elsewhere is the call,' she said, as one man, we both rose to leave.

A look of panic crossed Clive's face. 'You don't have to commit yourself right now, just put your thumbprint on the bottom of this page to say you're still interested,' he shouted after us.

I turned at the door for one last look at the defeated Clive, who was talking a handful of tablets, I knew exactly how he felt having been there many times before. Live and learn but some, like myself, just live.

COBBER'S TALE
Eve Mugford

In the year nineteen hundred and fourteen when Edward Cobbs was a young, strong man he was recruited to fight for his country at war. Two years later he was seriously wounded in France and discharged out of the army to recover his health and civilian life again.

Cobber's injuries were severe and when repaired . . . left his body rigid from the neck to the knees . . . locked solid . . . with a damaged spine and many pieces of shrapnel from enemy shells still scattered throughout his body.

His obvious handicap earned him much admiration in the town where he lived and the girls flocked to soothe and flirt with the young, handsome hero as he lay on an invalid bed in the sunshine of his garden to recuperate.

As his injuries healed, Edward learned to shuffle, walk and wooden backed he propelled himself with small precise steps . . . rocking from side to side and supported by two heavy walking sticks. Stiff-faced and with his chin frozen into many muscular ridges as it pressed down onto his neck in the effort to see his lower body . . . Cobber progressed . . . and made many adjustments to his daily survival.

Pretty Peggy Batten won his heart finally and they married, remaining childless until she died at forty-three leaving him lost and lonely without her tireless vitality.

Cobber managed to survive after her death . . . but oh so badly! He found the daily misery of dressing himself appalling and his body became sore and bruised with his many falls. The task of dragging on and off his high-waisted trousers . . . using the crook ends of his two sticks as aids . . . was sheer torment! It took him so long to slip on his special boots that often utter weariness and despair exhausted him.

Now in his middling years, his handicap had etched deep lines of stress and suffering on his still handsome face and the veins on his hands and arms had become swollen and knotted with overuse in supporting his stiffened body.

Edward Cobbs lived next door to the Meeden family and he was such a quiet man that although they were neighbours . . . close friendship had never developed between them.

However . . . one day a startling announcement of Hilda Meeden's completely astonished her family when she declared that she would take over caring for Cobber 'as good training for becoming a nurse'. Her stunned parents' protests at their fifteen year old daughter's outburst fell on deaf ears . . . she was determined in her resolve.

Displaying a clinical detachment never before realised by her family, the young girl washed, shaved and helped dress Cobber every morning, repeating some of the same process at night, before she went home to her own bed.

At first, as she was so determined in her task, father accompanied her and sat talking to Cobber while she attended to him, but Hilda's professional attitude calmed any delicate fears that he'd had and so the girl carried on alone and he worried no more.

Fate took a hand in determining the invalid's future and one day something happened to Cobber that was to change his life completely. The day began very hot, it was breathless, bathed in molten sunlight and even the birds looked fatigued and lazed sleepily in the shrubs in the small back garden.

'Good morning Mr Cobbs,' Hilda greeted the hapless man, pinned solidly to his narrow bed and iron hard mattress by his affliction. 'It's a clean shirt this morning, up we come now' and aided by Cobber hooking his sticks around the bed frame, Hilda manoeuvred her patient to a stiff leaning position on the edge of the bed.

'I'm looking forward to a nice walk this morning, to get out into the air Hilda, it's been so hot and close all night,' and Cobber allowed the girl to ease on his trousers over the ramrod legs and after slipping on the shirt she supported his back firmly while he manfully tucked it into his trousers, fastening the thick leather belt around them.

Thankfully Hilda completed his ablutions quickly and Cobber endured the painful embarrassing procedure without too much discomfort. While Edward Cobbs tended to his personal needs Hilda prepared his breakfast and then . . . checking all was well, she left, knowing that Cobber was to venture out later to do a little shopping.

Cobber eased himself down the shallow step from house to street and with knees locked, he began his pendulous shuffle forward, leaning heavily on the walking sticks and slowly . . . he made his way to the shop at the top of the road.

'Morning Mr Cobbs . . . how's it with you today then?' Ivy Barker, wife of the shop owner greeted him cheerfully as she busily wrapped apples and tomatoes.
'Nicely thank you Ivy, mustn't complain,' he murmured politely.
'Shan't keep you a minute then dearie' and Ivy finished weighing new potatoes to slip into a customer's bag.

Cobber set himself to wait and started to self-consciously count the oranges stacked in a fancy display in the side window of the shop. Suddenly, the woman in front of him swayed backwards and with hands clutching her head, she crumpled and fell heavily against him.

'Oh my gawd, grab her someone, she's going orf,' shouted Ivy and dropping the heavy brass pan she lunged towards the stricken woman.

Luckily the lady toppled backwards against Cobber, who was already steady and solid in his stance and moaning softly she slid down to the floor to lay in an unconscious heap.

It was Ivy and another customer who carried the woman into a room at the back of the shop and administered Sol Volatile and smelling salts to revive her while Cobber anxiously waited . . . feeling ashamed that he'd been unable to help the woman himself.

Later that evening when the enduring Hilda's help with his night time ablutions Cobber related the morning's incident to her.

'Useless . . . young Hilda . . . that's how I felt and that poor woman had to lay there at my feet until someone else could lift her up. It was humiliating,' and Edward Cobb's face was vulnerable in his anger.
'Now then, don't take on so Mr Cobbs, it couldn't be helped, you did your best, in fact the lady could have fallen very heavily and cracked her head if you hadn't been there to cushion her fall, think on that if you

will!' and Hilda placed thick cheese sandwiches and a large cup of cocoa consolingly in front of the sad man, for his supper.

Before going to her own bed that night, young Hilda confided poor Cobber's misery to her parents and they discussed the possible merit of his going into a soldier's home for the war wounded where he would get the companionship and confidence that he sorely needed.

Several days passed by and Cobber needed to shop for vegetables again. Ivy greeted him as usual then suddenly rushed into the back room and returned with a letter which she held out to the surprised man. 'Oh Mr Cobbs, I'm glad you called, there's this note for you, it's been here nearly a week now and it was left by the lady that fainted in here,' she tucked the envelope into his jacket pocket to save him relinquishing the hold on his sticks.

Having made his purchases and once more safely indoors again Cobber opened the letter. It was quaintly worded and very formal and thanked the 'kind man who had buffered her fall' and explained that having just recovered from a bout of pneumonia she had foolishly ventured out too soon, weakness had overcome her and so she had collapsed. The letter went on to apologise for any discomfort that she may have caused him and signed off . . . with my sincere gratitude Eva Gray.

The letter pleased Cobber for two reasons, firstly, because he never ever got any letters at all and next, because he'd actually been useful to someone. He read and re-read the simple note with great satisfaction.

Once again fate took a hand through Hilda and her ambitions for when Cobber showed her the letter, as conclusive evidence to his previous news, she noted the woman's address and vowed to call on her to see if she needed any help to further her nurse's training programme.

By the end of the week she had made contact with Mrs Gray and the startled woman at first surprised by Hilda's appearance at her house, soon warmed to the young girl's obvious sincerity and as she got to know her better, they became good friends.

Eva Gray was incredibly thin and undernourished and it was nothing short of a miracle that Hilda intervened when she did to help her recovery to good health again. As for the girl, she now had two patients to care for and with the strong support from her family behind her, they both progressed very well.

Kate and Gordon Meeden decided that it was high time they all got together and so they invited Cobber and Eva to tea one Saturday afternoon. Their small girl Rosie and baby Alice kept the atmosphere easy and informal and soon the two guests were chatting away together like close friends.

Eva Gray became a regular visitor and friend to the Meeden household and she eventually confided her life story to Kate, one afternoon as the women made gooseberry jam together.

'This preserve looks delicious Kate, it reminds me of the golden brandied plums my own mother used to prepare for the Yuletide celebrations,' murmured Eva as she stirred the simmering liquid.

'Where did you live Eva? Was it Germany or Switzerland?' asked Kate carefully.

'In Germany. Has that upset your dear friend to know I'm from the country that you've suffered a bloody war with?' and Eva searched her face for any hatred or disgust.

'But you married one of our soldiers who brought you home to England as his bride . . . surely you don't think we would hate you? Especially now that poor Robert is dead and you are all alone,' protested Kate. 'Oh Eva, don't think that all the world is against you or else you'll never find happiness again. Why, our Hilda is now positive that you are getting stronger, so don't get run down again, we all like you,' and Kate squeezed the woman's arm reassuringly.

'I have suffered much hatred and rudeness from being the German wife of an English Tommy, I've been spat upon and pushed over when out shopping, but then Robert was alive to comfort me,' Eva whispered sadly.

With Hilda as their chaperon Eva and Cobber met quite often now at each other's houses or at the Meeden's and it wasn't long before the wonderful solution to their individual problems occurred to them both.

And so they were married. A small but very happy wedding reception was held at the Meeden's house with their other 'side' neighbours, dear Jock and Maggie McPherson. Ivy Barker and her husband Solly completing the guests attending and it was truly an emotional and tender celebration.

Kate and Maggie were so pleased to have gained another good friend and neighbour alongside them in Eva and it was Hilda's reward for all her capable caring to see the blossoming of two lonely people into such a joyful partnership together.

A WORM'S TALE
Eric Holt

'Do you like gardening?'
The little girl looked up at Sam as he leaned on his spade, taking a breather after a hard slog of digging. He was turning over a little used patch of soil on his small allotment in preparation for the coming spring.

Sam looked down at the little girl. She was, he guessed, about six, not particularly pretty, with curly blonde hair. She wore a non-descript blue dress, and white socks. Brown sandals completed her attire.
'Sometimes,' answered Sam, 'when I've not so much digging to do.'
'Why do you dig?'
The little girl looked up into his face with her piercing blue eyes. Her eyes were the most unusual feature. Very wise in such a young face. Deep, almost, one could say, unfathomable.
'Why do I dig?' chucked Sam, 'I can just see this lot if I didn't. I've got to break up the soil so as I can put some seeds and plants in later on. It won't dig itself, you know!'

The little girl thought for a moment, then said, 'Why don't you let the worms turn the soil over for you.'
Sam laughed out loud, 'I know that worms move the soil about a bit, but it would take a long, long time and a great army of worms to make anything of this lot.'
The little girl shook her head. 'Not if you asked them to bring all their friends and work fast,' she said, seriously.
'Oh, yes!' exploded Sam, 'I can just see myself talking to worms. Imagine, eh! Now, worms, listen to me. Let's have some action, and don't wriggle when I'm talking to you. Right, shift that soil - bury them leaves - come on - come on - quicker, quicker! Dear, dear! Talk to worms, indeed!'

He chortled as he ruffled the little girl's hair with his rough gardener's hand.
'I can ask them if you want,' she said, 'they always listen to me.'
Old Sam looked down at the little girl, a wide grin splitting his leathery, weather-beaten face. 'Do they now?' he exclaimed, 'And how come you're their special friend, eh?'

'I don't know,' she answered, shaking her head, slowly, 'I've always been able to talk to animals and birds and all crawly things. I tell wasps to go out of our kitchen, cos my mum doesn't like them. They go away, always.'

The little girl looked so sincere that Sam thought it wouldn't do any harm to humour her so he said, 'Okay then I'll let you talk to my worms, and, if they do a good job for me, I'll give you ten pence for some toffees. How does that sound, alright?'
Nodding her head, sagely, the little girl knelt on the path which ran through the centre of the allotment. Placing her small face very close to the ground, she began to mutter in a soft monotone. Sam couldn't hear any definite words, but, from the tone, he could sense that the child was coaxing and cajoling.

It was evident that she was sincere. Her concentration was absolute. Sam held his breath, afraid to break the spell. A strange silence descended on the allotment. Even the traffic sounds from the main road where stilled. There was no birdsong. Time hung, suspended, in the quiet air. It could not have been more than a few minutes, yet, to Sam it seemed as if he had been listening to the child for hours. Eventually, with a sigh, the little girl raised herself, rocked back on her heels, looked at Sam, and smiled. 'They'll do it,' she said, simply, 'they didn't want to at first, but they'll do it.'

She stayed very still, and Sam was just about to say something when the words froze on his lips. As he looked down at the unturned soil the whole surface began to heave as in a miniature earthquake! The soil fairly bubbled! Worms, hundreds, thousands, wriggled and writhed to the surface! They burrowed out of sight only to reappear in mad mix of stirring soil. Heavy clods of clay disintegrated into soft loam. The top dressing of old compost sank and became part of the deposit of crumbly loam.

In five minutes the unreal, almost nightmarish, activity had stopped. Every centimetre of Sam's patch had been turned over and over. Strangely, there was not a single worm in sight.

Sam was shaken to the core! He had never seen anything like it in all his sixty-six years. He just could not believe it. Furthermore, he was sure no one else would believe it, that is, if he should be daft enough to mention it to anybody.

The little girl stood up, brushed her knees with her hands, and smiled at Sam. 'They nearly always do it, when I ask them to.' she said, in a matter-of-fact way. Then she held out her hand. Sam looked down at the outstretched palm, shook himself, and reached into his pocket. He brought out a ten pence piece. Changing his mind, he brought out a handful of coins, selected two ten pence pieces and placed them in the little girl's hand.

She grinned at him, turned, and skipped away. A sparrow flew down and landed on her shoulder. She laughed with pleasure, spoke to the bird, and pointed to Sam. Then she disappeared behind the tall privet hedge.

Sam knelt on the path, his strong fingers crumbled a handful of the loamy soil. Had he dreamt all this happening? Had he, himself, dug the soil, and then had some kind of a memory black-out? After all, it was a hot day, and he was no spring chicken. Perhaps it was a warning to take things easy.

He stood up, shaking his grey head, determined to think no more about the little girl, the worms, and the memory lapse. He turned to pick up his spade. He caught his breath! There on the path, glistening in the sunlight were two ten pence pieces!

THE BOY
Paddy Jupp

Curiouser and curiouser and it gets more so the older I become. Call it an old lady's whim that I need to tell you now because I've never told anyone else although it's happened several times over the years.

It began when I was nine or ten and saw him running across the field behind the house - a young boy, dark-haired, sallow skinned and about two years younger than me. I wondered who he was but decided he must be staying on holiday with relatives in the village as I didn't recognise him. I didn't see him again and put him out of my mind.

However, he reappeared when I was in my late teens at the Ilford Palais one Saturday night and I thought how good-looking he was. He looked straight at me for long seconds and I expected him to come over so I dropped my eyes, waiting for him to ask me to dance but when I looked up again he had vanished. It was most disturbing.

After that, a few years passed when I married and brought up a family but the young man's image never really faded.

Then, around nineteen seventy-six, I was shopping in Romford market and dropped my purse. Before I could retrieve it a gentleman of middle years like me, bent to pick it up but was beaten to it by a younger woman who moved more quickly and handed it to me with a big smile whilst accepting my grateful thanks. I turned to also thank the gentleman but he was nowhere to be seen though I will always remember his very dark eyes which gazed into mine with an almost pleading look. It was eerie; he seemed so familiar.

It must have been around eighteen months ago when I saw him again. There was a new play which was having great reviews in London so I booked a ticket and took the train early one morning intending to sightsee a little before the matinee. On entering the carriage my only companion was an elderly man reading a newspaper in a corner seat who didn't look up when I sat down opposite him. As the train moved off I settled down to read my book but after a while I looked out of the window and got the fright of my life for reflecting back at me was the man's face which was so very like my own. It made me tremble so violently I almost ran down the carriage away from the apparition, desperately willing the next station to materialise so I could get off the train and as far away from the man as possible, for he made my flesh creep. I almost threw myself on to the platform and looked back to make sure he wasn't following me, but there was no one there.

That was when I started trying to find my elder sister for I had the strongest feeling she might be able to help me. Although the family had split up years ago and we children were put into care, I managed eventually to trace her to the West Country. She wasn't keen to see me but after much persuasion agreed to a meeting and my intuition had been right.

She told me that my mother had given birth to a child two years after me but it had only lived for a few hours.

The baby was a boy.

AND SO GOD CREATED EARTH
Robert Gerald

A long time ago the heavens and skies were ruled by God with the help of his loyal subjects - the Sun, Moon, Clouds, Rain, Stars, and the terrible twins, Thor, God of Thunder, and Mars, God of War. He called them his 'soldiers of the sky'.

The Sun and Moon often stayed up late talking and by next morning, the Sun was too tired to shine and his friend the Moon would be very irritable. Now the Stars were always causing trouble and they told the Moon that it was the Sun's fault that he was so miserable so the two friends would quarrel.

Thor and Mars were always quarrelling and were pleased to see others in similar trouble.

Now Rain and Clouds were so upset about these quarrels that they complained to God, who scolded the culprits, and though they promised to behave, in no time they were fighting once more.

So God decided to separate the friends and told Sun that in future he would shine for twelve hours, and this was called 'Day' and Moon would shine for the other twelve hours and this would be 'Night'. Since Sun did not have to compete with Moon, he shone with such warmth and brightness that 'daytime' became a pleasant time.

Poor old Moon could not shine as bright as the Sun and even though his friendly Stars helped him, the 'night-time' was much darker than day. Sometimes at night the Twins would use their strong breath to blow Cloud across the skies making it very dark and the Moon and Stars could not be seen. The breath of the Twins was called the Wind.

Occasionally this happened during daytime but the Clouds could not hide the strong rays of the Sun for long.

This arrangement meant that the two friends only had a fleeting glance of each other in the morning and late evening.

One morning just as Cloud and Rain were saying 'hello' to the two friends they noticed a strange object in the sky.
Cloud said 'I've never seen that before,'

And Rain replied, 'It looks just like the Sun and the Moon.'
Just then God spoke, 'That is the planet Earth that I've created' and he told Sun, 'I want you to shine your warmth upon it every day, whilst Cloud must carry Rain and drop him lightly on the Earth's surface.'

Every day his three soldiers carried out their new roles and soon the Earth began to look very green. Cloud was curious and went down to investigate and on his return he reported that the Earth's surface was covered with some kind of green substance and everywhere there were tall objects, but he did not know the reason for this.

God heard them and said, 'What you see are green fields of grass and trees, and if you carry on your good work, soon there will be other colours appearing such as blue, red, yellow and white, and these will be flowers.'
True enough this is what happened.

They still wondered why Earth had been created and God read their thoughts and replied, 'Soon there will be water everywhere which will be known as rivers, lakes and seas. You will also see large numbers of creatures who will feed on the lush green grass. There will be birds that fly in the sky, animals who will walk on four legs, fish swimming in the water, and insects and reptiles of all kinds.'

So it came about that there were tame animals of all shapes and sizes - cattle, horses, sheep, pigs, goats, deer, also wild animals like wolves, elephants, tigers, lions, large and small wild birds such as robins, sparrows, blackbirds, eagles and hawks. Similarly there were reptiles and insects, and large and small creatures that swam in the water. There were such a lot of creatures, too many to mention.

By now, Earth was a peaceful 'paradise' of tame and wild creatures, but not for long for they began to quarrel amongst each other.

Once again God had to find a solution to the problem and eventually decided to create something more intelligent, and this creature was called 'Man' and he walked upright on two legs. His name was Adam and it was his job to keep the other creatures under control.

However, the creatures began to multiply and as a result there were constant quarrels. Adam found it impossible to carry out his work, so he appealed to God who promised to do something about it. The next day he found a satisfactory answer, by sending some of the creatures such as the bears, wolves, fox and walrus to the north, to be known as the Northern Hemisphere; others such as the penguins, albatross, kangaroos, koala bears and emus he sent to the south - the Southern Hemisphere; and some to the Earth's centre, such as parrots, lions, tigers, and elephants which became known as the Equatorial area. It seemed a perfect solution.

Years went by and from the sky the Earth looked beautiful and peaceful, now that all the creatures had been spread around.

However, Adam became very sad and told God, 'I feel very lonely,' whereupon God said, 'If you give up one of your ribs, I will find you a mate,'
Adam felt that he would not miss one rib, so he willingly agreed.

Next morning he discovered a beautiful person by his side who was like him, but so divine that the sight took his breath away. This was 'Woman' and her name was Eve.

Adam was now quite happy and soon he and Eve had two children named Cain and Abel. At last God felt that his job on Earth was done.

Meanwhile the 'soldiers of the sky' carried on with their daily work, all except the terrible twins, who still quarrelled over who should blow Cloud around the skies.

Poor Cloud was unhappy about the situation, especially the heavy task of carrying Rain around with him, and often in despair he would suddenly drop Rain and Earth would be drenched in a heavy shower.

One day as the Twins fought, their shields clashed with a loud rumble, and when their swords touched there was a bright, blinding light. This we call 'Thunder and Lightning'. Cloud was blown all over the place, and in fright he dropped Rain who fell, but this time it was so cold that Rain had frozen and Earth was pelted with small lumps of ice. These we know as 'Hailstones'.

Whenever there was Thunder and Lightning, Eve would run and hide, and even after the Rain had stopped she was afraid to come out, and

Adam had to comfort her. In despair she asked Adam to talk to God to see if he could do something about it.

Once more Adam appealed to God who promised to remedy the matter. Thereupon he gave the Twins a good scolding and though they promised to behave, he knew that because of their quarrelsome nature it would certainly happen again.

Nevertheless he promised Eve that the next time there was Thunder and Lightning he would send a 'sign' to show that he was dealing with the matter. This sign was the 'Rainbow' - an arc of beautiful colours in the sky, and to this day whenever we see a Rainbow we know that the rain will soon stop and the Sun will shine again.

Eve was reassured but not for long, for she was forever looking for ways to improve their daily life.

It was a month later when she said to Adam, 'Do you realise it is difficult to know when Day has finished and Night has begun, for the change comes so quickly. Couldn't you talk to God about it?'

Adam was by now annoyed by Eve's constant moaning, so he told her 'Don't you think that God might have had enough of our requests?'
But she persisted and he thought to himself perhaps this will be the last time. So he appealed to God one more time saying, 'Why does the Sun rise and the Moon set so quickly without any warning? Couldn't you find a solution?'

It so happened that God realised that it would take a long time to make the Earth perfect, and after much deliberation he found a satisfactory answer. He said 'In future, Night will gradually fade away as the Sun creeps into the sky, this will be known as 'Dawn'. Similarly, at night as the Sun slowly slips away it will get darker a little at a time until it is Night once more. This period before darkness will be called 'Dusk'.

All these changes we have come to accept as part of our daily life.

ROBBERY AT THE FACE
Michael John Swain

Word was out that Hickton main colliery was being closed by the present government. Those employees with years of service in would receive golden handshakes. But for Steve, Mac and his two sons Phil and Adam there would be nothing, as they had only just relocated from London.

The situation looked bad. More so as Steve's mother needed a life-saving operation which could only be performed by a world specialist living in Switzerland and costing £40,000 kronas and needed to be performed in the next six months if she was to have any chance of survival.

That evening Steve, Mac, Adam and Phil had an emergency meeting in Mac's conservatory to discuss the situation. The sound of beer cans popping broke the silence as the meeting got under way.

Steve was in the chair and spoke first. 'I propose that we draw up a plan to grab the colliery redundancy payroll which is worth 4 million pounds.'
It all went quiet as Steve's words echoed home. 4 million pounds.
Mac spoke next. 'What's the split then brother?'
Steve looked up with his steely grey eyes fixed straight at Mac. 'A four way split. 1 million each.'
Phil and Adam gasped. 1 million each. Was this for real or just a dream?
Steve eyed the group one by one, 'Anyone who wants out can go now with no hard feelings. We all have wives and if caught can expect at least 15 years each without remission.'
Adam spoke next. 'We all have some years of unionship under our belts so let's sleep on it, meet again same time tomorrow and take a vote on it.'
'That sounds logical to me,' said Steve, 'All agreed?'
They all agreed, finished their beers and left.

Next evening arrived and the four met up again. Steve took charge of the proceedings. 'I hereby propose that all those present take part in grabbing the colliery payroll. If agreed, raise your right hand.'

Three hands shot high in the air. Steve's normally granite iron steely face broke into a wry smile. 'Whatever we discuss stays in this conservatory. Do not speak to anyone or we will all go down together.' The trio nodded their acknowledgement.

'Right,' said Steve, 'now down to some serious planning. The final payroll redundancy payments are due to be delivered a week on Thursday. That gives us ten days to rehearse the robbery and iron out any snags.' Steve then handed all three an A4 sheet of paper. 'Whatever is written down you will need to memorise as no papers leave this conservatory. 'Now,' carried on Steve, 'for the last six weeks on my day off I have, through the eyes of a pair of binoculars, observed the delivery of the weekly payroll, and this is the result. One armed truck is involved. Three guards. Two in the front. One in the rear of the truck. The arrival time varies each week by approximately 20 minutes before or past the hour, on a regular pattern, but always in the morning. On arrival one of the guards on his radio rings back to base everything is okay. After about 5 minutes one of the guards leaves the truck, gives four large taps on the colliery door followed by two short taps then four large taps. Then he is admitted inside. Once inside, he uses his mobile phone to tell his two mates it's safe to bring the money in. Whilst he keeps watch from the doorway the two guards load up the sacks of money on a pallet board which is then pulled inside the collier doors. Any questions?'

Phil raises his hand. 'Approximately how long does it take to load up the pallet?'

'Seven minutes and twenty-eight seconds,' replied Steve. 'Anyway, here's the plan. We all have gasmasks as issued by the pit, but first we put on black balaclavas then the gasmask followed by army jumpers and army denims. Black rubber boots, black rubber gloves, four cans of CS gas, no firearms. That way no one can get shot. Next Saturday Leeds are playing at home. Our cover is we are all going to the match. Wear your supporter's scarves, that way no one will be suspicious. We take Mac's car as that is the biggest one. Cycles in the back. Leaving here at 11.00am. Prompt.'

They all nodded their approval.

That evening Mac told Sue his wife that he Phil, Adam and Steve were off to Leeds on Saturday for the big match.

Sue seemed pleased. 'That's fine by me,' she replied, 'I will ask Joy, Carrie and Lena over and we can have a bit of a girl's party and get together.'

Mac laughed, he had heard all about Sue's supposedly parties. Knicker parties.

Saturday morning had arrived and Mac and Sue usually had a nice long lie in bed as working on shifts at the pit made home life a little difficult. Mac had been up early, shaved, and showered, and was now parading round the bedroom in just his underpants smelling of aftershave, talc and bodyspray. He sat on the edge of the bed and stroked Sue's long blonde hair, a smile broke on her face and her lips pouted. She half sat up, her firm taut breasts falling just over the top of the sheets exposing her elongated nipples. She kissed Mac gently on the lips. 'Don't go to the silly match darling. Stay in bed with me,' she purred.

Any other time Mac would have obliged, but with a stake of one million in the offing he declined his wife's offer. 'Sorry sweetheart, I promised the lads and I'm driving the car. Anyway you won't be alone, the girls are coming over and I will expect you to tell me all about it. Knickers and all.' Giving Sue a quick kiss, Mac left.

He pipped the car as he drove out of the garage. Steve, Adam and Phil were all ready when Mac called for them and the party set off in earnest. Mac switched the radio off as Steve said 'Right, let's get to it.' 'Okay Mac' said Steve, 'drive to Marton Quarry. It's about three miles off the motorway slip road by Burston Bridge.'

'I know where you mean,' replied Mac.

The tension in the car was electric as the four drove towards the quarry. No one spoke. Mac slowed down and applied the brakes as the quarry loomed in view.

'Everyone out.' said Steve, 'By the way no one works at the quarry at the weekend. I've checked it out.'

They all lined up beside the car, whilst Steve fetched two black holdalls from the boot of the car.

'Right,' said Steve, 'this is a one off rehearsal. So we must get it right first time. No mistakes, okay?'

The trio nodded. Steve handed each one a black balaclava, a black jumper, gasmask, army denims, rubber gloves, rubber shoes, CS gas. 'Let's dress the part.'

They all changed clothes.
'First I want you all to imagine that Mac's car is the payroll delivery truck. It has just arrived and is parked outside the colliery main office block.'
The rehearsal was a big success and they headed home.

Wednesday evening, prior to the big day, they all met in Mac's conservatory going through the whole operation to clear up any problems.

Thursday, D Day, this was it. The payroll arrived as usual. On Steve's signal they went into action. Mac came round the corner on his cycle, drove at the security guards, squirting CS gas into his eyes. At the same time, Phil and Adam did the same to the two guards loading up the pallet with the payroll.

Steve drove up and they all helped to put the payroll into Mac's car. In no time they were loaded up. Mac drove the armoured truck. Steve drove Mac's car and they all sped off at great speed.

Shortly afterwards both vehicles pulled up at the south face of the mine. Their hands ripped at the boards holding the concealed entrance to the disused mine shaft. Long extinct. They soon transferred the payroll into the disused shaft. Taking extra care to board it up again. Then they drove off at great speed and upon reaching a secluded woodland area lost no time in setting fire to the armoured truck, burning all their clothes. Cycles were taken from Mac's car and they set off in different directions. Except for Mac who made his way home in his car.

Next day. Headlines in the paper were 'Outside gang robs colliery payroll. Police investigation. 4 million stolen.'
They all met up as prearranged in Mac's conservatory. 'Well done everyone,' said Steve. 'No one got hurt and we got the cash. We will let it stay underground for four months, agreed?'
They all agreed. Steve more than anyone, as now he could afford to send his mum for that vital operation.

IT KEEPS THINGS EVEN
Derek Wheatley

Jim Sullivan parked his car on the promenade, mid-way between the two piers, he looked up at the parking signs, the restrictions were still in force. He got a ticket from the Pay and Display machine. 25th September, 3 o'clock in the afternoon. Bitter cold it was, just like his wedding day 20 years ago, 'unseasonal', they said. Bloody freezing more like. It probably explained why there weren't many people around. He walked across to one of the shelters on the seafront to escape from the wind. He sat down to read the paper he'd bought from the kiosk nearby.

Twenty years had past since he was last here, on his honeymoon with his childhood sweetheart, Jane. They'd stopped at the north end, it was cheaper there, they hadn't been able to afford much but she had insisted on getting married, a headstrong girl was Jane but he loved her all the same, he couldn't imagine himself being with anyone else, '2.4 children we'll have,' she'd say, 'and a semi and we'll all live happily ever after'.

Sadly though it wasn't to be. 'Blocked fallopian tubes,' the doctor said. 'Unable to conceive', so she'd thrown herself into her job as a nursery nurse to be near other people's kids, torturing herself he thought.

She'd have loved to have brought one home yet she wouldn't even consider adoption. 'If it's meant to be it's meant to be', she'd say.

Still he wouldn't have minded a child, whichever way, they'd been happy enough though with their hobbies, holidays and making their home nice.

Then the accident happened, not long after her 38th birthday. A hit and run accident, on a zebra crossing of all places. 18 months had passed and he'd tried everything to break the depression. He missed Jane terribly and wanted to be with her, that's why he'd come here today. He'd wait till midnight and then do a Reggie Perrin, only he would swim out to sea and not come back, it wouldn't take long, he thought, he wasn't a strong swimmer and the water would be cold.

'Hello Mister. What are you doing here?'

He looked around and there stood a little blonde-haired girl about seven.

'My name's Julie. What's yours?'

'Jim,' he said.

'How old are you?'

'38,' he replied.

'I'm seven,' she said. 'My dad calls me Jewels but Grandad calls me his little treasure because he always buries me in the sand. Have you come on holiday? Do you have any children? I'm looking for someone to play with, will you play with me?'

He laughed. 'Where's your mum and dad?' he asked.

'Down there on the beach,' she said, 'looking for our dog.'

'Do you live here?' he asked.

'Yes,' she replied. 'I'm staying with my gran across the road, she runs a boarding house.'

'Oh! Don't you think you ought to go back to your mum?'

'No, I'm alright here, they can see me,' she said, waving to the couple down the beach.

'Shall I take you to them?'

'If you buy me an ice-cream, I'll go back with you.'

'Alright then,' he said, getting up to go to the kiosk.

'Can I have a Ninety Nine please?'

He bought two and they walked down the steps towards the beach.

'Where do you come from?' she asked.

'Nottingham,' he replied.

'Where's your wife?' she asked.

'I haven't got one now, she died.'

'Every man should have a wife, my gran says, so it keeps things even.'

They got nearer to the couple.

'I hope she's not bothering you.'

'No, not at all. I'm just concerned, she was wandering about on her own, you know how things are these days, it's not really safe.'

'We are happy enough if we can see her, she usually makes friends with someone. We live just across the way, we run a boarding house with my mum 'Home from Home' it's called if you're looking for somewhere to stay.'

'Thanks all the same but I'm only here for the day.'

'Cheerio then.'
'Thanks for the ice-cream, mister.'
'You're welcome,' he said 'and I hope you find your dog.'

He walked up from the beach to the prom and headed towards the south pier. He looked for the places they'd visited all those years ago. Most things had changed, it was all arcades now and gift shops, anything to part you from your money. He was getting hungry, it had been a long drive from Nottingham and he hadn't eaten since breakfast. He went into a little cafe, it was empty except for the woman behind the counter.
'What would you like love?' she said.
'A plate of fish and chips please.'
'Bread and butter and a cup of tea?'
'Thanks. That would be nice.'

He sat waiting, looking out of the window, a little tap disturbed his thoughts. The blonde-haired little girl came in and sat opposite him at the table. 'Hello again,' Julie said.
'What are you doing here?' he asked.
'I always come here.' she said. 'What are you having to eat?' she asked.
'Fish and chips,' he replied. 'Would you like some?'
'No thanks, I'll just share yours. Mummy says eating between meals spoils my tea. I got told off for the ice-cream.'
'Oh! I'm sorry.'
'I'm not!' she said laughing.

The meal arrived and he started to eat, she occasionally reached across to take a chip between questions.
'Have you been here before?'
'Yes, a very long time ago.'
'I'm sorry your wife died.'
'So am I.'
'Did you love her?'
'Yes.'
'Lots?'
'Oh yes.'
'Will you find another?'
'I don't think so.'
'Shall we have a sweet?'

'I thought it would spoil your tea.'

'I'll just tell Mum I'm not hungry.'

'What would you suggest?'

'Apple pie and custard, you get lots!'

He turned to the woman behind the counter. 'Two apple pie and custards please. How much will I owe you?' He gave her a ten pound note.

'It won't be a minute love,' she said as she gave him his change.

'Shall I show you round after we've eaten?' the little girl said.

'If you like, but won't they be worried?'

'No,' she said. 'My mum will be helping Gran serve the guests and Dad will be washing-up and serving behind the bar.'

'What's the place called?' asked Jim.

'Home from Home. It's just round the corner from where I first saw you. Come on then let's go. She took hold of his hand and led him down the pier. He won her a little doll on the darts and a cuddly toy on the rifle range. It was quite late and very dark as they made their way back up the prom, he hadn't realised how far away he'd parked his car.

He could feel the rain spitting in the wind, he was warm enough but it hadn't occurred to him the little girl was only lightly dressed.

'Are you cold?' he asked.

'No, I'll be alright,' Julie replied, 'it's not far now.'

Without warning the heavens opened and a heavy burst of rain hit them. 'Quick!' she squealed. 'Run!' Grabbing his hand they ran for shelter in a bus stop. They made it just in time as the storm broke. Looking down, she said, 'Your laces are undone.'

'I'm not surprised!' he said. 'I haven't run so far so fast for a long time.' He stooped down to tie them. When he looked up she'd disappeared and the rain was still falling heavily. He ran to the corner of the street and collided with a very lightly built young woman. She fell to the ground as she bounced off him. He bent down to help her up. She was absolutely sodden.

'What the blazes.' said Angela.

'Are you alright?' he asked pulling her to her feet.

'No not really,' she said.

'Did you see a young girl, blonde hair, about seven?'

No,' she said. 'Look at me.'

He could see she was absolutely wet through, but glancing over her shoulder on the other side of the street, he saw a sign lit up 'Home from Home'. There was a light in the window to the right of the door, and the curtains were drawn. The street was deserted and the rain was still teeming down.

'Excuse me,' he said, 'give me a minute and I'll help sort you out.' He crossed the road and she followed him. He knocked on the door. After what seemed like an age an old lady leaning heavily on a walking stick opened it, she looked a good age, about 85.

'Come in.' she said, 'You're both wet through.'

They walked through a narrow passage into a small lounge, it felt warm and cosy. 'Would you like to sit down,' she said. 'What can I do for you?'

The young woman spoke up. 'Could you find me some dry clothes please and a towel, I'm wringing wet through. This fool pushed me into a puddle.'

'Come with me dear,' said Doris.

They went up some stairs and he was left to look round the neat little room, glancing at the photographs. There was one of the little girl who had befriended him and another of the couple he had seen on the beach, in the photograph, the black spaniel dog they were looking for was between them. Various other photos of the family and friends were spread around the room, but before he could look at them, the old lady came back down the stairs, she was followed into the room by the young woman, who was now wearing a dressing gown and a towel wrapped round her head.

He thought how attractive she looked and noticed her green eyes, he wondered if she'd got a jealous nature.

'Here you are young man, these belonged to my late husband, they might be a bit big, but they're dry. Go upstairs and leave your other clothes in the drying room.' Doris said.

He went to change. When he came back down Doris had poured out three cups of tea. The young woman stood up as he entered the room, she looked across at him.

'My name's Angela, Angela Davies.' She held out her hand.

'Pleased to meet you. My name's Jim, Jim Sullivan.'

'Oh! Don't you two know each other then?' said the old lady.
'Well, no not really, we just bumped into each other on the corner,' replied Angela, 'I was just looking for somewhere to shelter when this fool knocked me down.'
'Well my name's Doris, Doris Hurd. I thought you were together, does this mean I'll have to get two rooms ready then?'
'Well I'm certainly not sleeping with him!' she said indignantly.
'Right. Two rooms it is then,' she said. 'I'll leave you two to decide what you'd like to eat and I'll see what we can rustle up when I come back down.'
'There's only one problem,' stated the young woman.
'No,' said the old lady. 'Not today, we don't want any problems today.'
'Would you like me to give you a hand?' said Jim.
'You can if you wish,' said the old lady.
'I'll come too if I may,' said Angela.
'The more the merrier. It's a long time since I had paying guests,' said the old lady.
'That's the problem,' said Angela. 'I won't be able to pay, not yet anyway.'
'It's alright love, we'll sort it out later.'

They turned the heating on in the two bedrooms at the top of the stairs, and made the beds between them.
The bathroom's there if you need it,' said Doris pointing to the end of the passage with her stick. 'No luggage I see, both of you runaways?' she said with a smile. 'I dare say you've both got stories to tell.'
'Well I have actually,' said Angela.
'You can tell me whilst we get dinner ready,' said Doris.

She took them into the kitchen at the back of the house.
'I'm on my own and I haven't got much in,' she said. 'It's a long time since I had guests. I can do you some soup, a ham salad and I'll find a tin of fruit for afters if you like.'
'That'll do fine,' said Jim.
'I'm starving,' said Angela. 'I haven't eaten all day. I left Nottingham this morning.'
'I'm from Nottingham,' he interrupted.
'Hush,' said Doris.

'I left Nottingham this morning,' said Angela again. 'God knows how I ended up here. I work at the hospital and my best friend has just died of cancer. I felt I had to go somewhere, anywhere. I've been working all hours and looking after her as well. I'm on my own now and I just snapped. I felt so alone, I never knew my parents. I was found in a wash room 21 years ago, I was raised in an orphanage, the nurse who found me at the hospital used to come and visit me, she was the only family I've ever had. They named me after her and when I left the orphanage I took her surname and went to stop with her. She was like a mother to me and now she's gone. Now I've got no one and nothing, I just climbed on a bus and ended up here. I've spent what money I had, and was looking for someone to help me when this fool knocked me over. I can send you what I owe you when I get back to Nottingham.'

'It's alright love,' Doris said. 'We'll sort that out later.'

'Now young man, what's your story?' asked Doris as they sat down to eat.

'Well,' he said, 'I'm ashamed to say I came here for a swim, I was going to kill myself.'

'Well that would have been a dumb, stupid thing to do,' said the old lady.

'I know,' he said.

'What's changed your mind then?'

'Well nothing really,' he said, 'it's just that I haven't got around to doing it yet.' He went on to tell his story and how much he loved his wife, he wanted to mention the little girl in the photo but he thought better of it.

'Right. I'll wash and you wipe,' said Angela. 'Doris can sit here and relax. We've got to do something to earn our keep.'

They went into the kitchen to do the pots discussing the different areas where they lived, their jobs and interests. When they came back into the lounge he felt he had known her for a long time.

Doris in the meantime had got a family photo album out, along with some glasses and a bottle of brandy. 'Come on,' she said, 'I think you could both do with a tot, it's been a long day. Now I'll tell you my story,' she said taking a sip. 'Cheers!'

She opened the album to show them her family photos, her husband in younger days, a handsome looking man, he'd died about 10 years ago. Two daughters, Jenny and Janice and their respective husbands. Then she got to the photo of the little girl, her name was Julie. Jim felt the hairs stand up on the back of his neck and a shiver went through him.

'She was my granddaughter, lovely little thing, she was always full of fun, it broke our hearts when she got washed out to sea.'

Jim went cold and tried to suppress a shudder. The gas fire was on and the room warm but for some reason he'd gone all clammy and a cold sweat broke out from his forehead.

Doris continued. 'Twenty-one years ago today, since it happened, she always went with her dad to walk the dog (Blackie, a little spaniel) before she went to bed. It weren't a very nice night and the wind was howling and the sea was very rough, after they had crossed the road she ran off in front of her dad as she often did, she climbed on the railings to watch the waves, before he could draw level with her a freak wave crashed over her and swept her out to sea, her dad was knocked off his feet and the dog ran off.

By the time he'd got up, there was no sign of her. He called the police and the coast guard but there was nothing anyone could do. They never found her body, so maybe, one day she may come back, that's my hope anyway.' With this she took a sip of brandy and wiped away a little tear. 'The dog came back on his own, still with the lead fastened to his collar, he bumped at the front door and ran off when we opened it. He was never seen again, pedigree he was, so someone had a good dog whoever found him. It broke our hearts. My daughter and son-in-law couldn't abide staying here after that. To have to pass the spot every day where they lost her. They went looking for a new home down south. Three months later they were killed on the motorway when a lorry jack-knifed. The insurance money from the accident paid for this place and we never took guests in again after that, it didn't seem right somehow. It made an old man out of my husband, he was never the same again, it was as if a light had gone out of his life and in a way it had. I'd never move away in case Julie ever came back, but that's just wishful thinking I suppose. Anyway, it's time for bed now you two, have a good lie in and I'll shout you for breakfast, but not too early.'

'Why did you take us in?' said Jim. 'When you don't take guests.'

'I couldn't be turning you away in weather like that,' said Doris. 'It wouldn't be right.'

'Thanks Doris,' said Angela kissing her on the cheek. 'You're an angel.'

'Well they come in many disguises,' said Doris. 'Goodnight, my room's down here.' With that she went to bed with another glass of brandy.

Angela and Jim climbed the stairs, she turned at the door and kissed him gently on the cheek. 'Goodnight,' she said.

'My door's got a lock on.' he said.

'So has mine,' she laughed, 'and I'm using it.' With that she shut the door.

Jim climbed into bed trying to make sense of the day's events, but he just faded into a deep sleep. It must have been the brandy because the next thing he heard, he was being called for breakfast.

Angela was already there, smartly dressed, Doris had ironed all her clothes, she looked really beautiful when she smiled.

'You can use my husband's shaving gear when you've had breakfast, we'll wash up,' said Doris.

His clothes were piled up on a chair neatly ironed, Doris must have got up really early. He went up the stairs after breakfast, he shaved and changed. When he came back down they were waiting in the lounge, he sensed they had been talking about him, they stopped as he walked in.

'Right,' said Doris, 'I suggest you two stop here for the weekend and get to know each other better, everybody needs somebody, it keeps things even. Now get out and enjoy yourselves, have a walk round and I'll see you later and don't worry about the bill.'

They walked down the street to the corner, he wanted to retrace his steps of yesterday, hoping someone else might have seen the little girl. He caught sight of his car, he'd better move it before he got a parking ticket. When he got there the traffic warden had already been, he'd move it later. They crossed to the kiosk. 'Excuse me,' said Jim. The man turned round, it wasn't the same one as yesterday.

'Yes Sir?' he said.

'Excuse me, where would I find the man who was here yesterday?'

'He's gone home mate, it's the end of the season, most folks have gone home now. Can I help you?'

'No not really.' He turned to Angela. 'Would you like anything?'

'Can I have a Ninety Nine please?'

Again he bought two.

'Shall we walk down the beach?' he said.

'I'd rather not in these shoes,' she said. 'Let's go down to the pier.'

'A good idea,' he said, pleased it was her suggestion. As they walked he kept looking round hoping he might see someone from yesterday, but there were even less people about now.

They came to the little cafe. 'Let's go in here for a drink,' he said.

She was glad to get out of the wind, it was really quite nippy, he went to the counter, a young girl about sixteen came to serve him, his heart sank.

'Two teas please.'

'Hello young man, I'm pleased you found some company.' It was the older woman from yesterday.

(He suddenly recognised her as Doris' other daughter Janice from the photos, he wondered at the coincidence.)

'By the way, you left your paper, I've saved it for you.'

'Thank you.' he said.

'You looked down in the dumps yesterday. I'm pleased you've got some company.'

'Yes, we've just met.'

'Excuse me,' he added, 'but have you worked here long, only I seem to think I know you from somewhere?'

'Oh, I come in to help a friend,' she said. 'I used to run a boarding house with my husband for the last 15 years but it's getting a bit too much now so I just work part time, maybe you stayed with us once?'

'Hardly,' he said. 'It's only my second visit in 20 years. When I came in yesterday you didn't see a young girl did you, about seven years old with blonde hair?'

'No Sir, but you did seem preoccupied and you must have been hungry because you ate two helpings of apple pie and custard, least ways both dishes were empty when I collected them in.'

He took the two teas back to the table.

'You look puzzled,' said Angela.

'It's nothing,' he said. 'I'm just thinking.'

'You've never been here before then?' he asked

'No,' she replied. 'I'm more used to walking in the Derbyshire hills. my mother and I as I called her, would drive to a pub car park and then we'd do a circular walk back in time for lunch or tea depending on the length of the walk, the fresh air used to do us good after working in a hospital all week, but it certainly doesn't feel as cold up in the hills as it does here, it must be because we are near the sea.'

They drank up and left the cafe. He wanted to go to the pier, when they got there two big gates were fastened and a sign saying 'Closed for redecoration, re-opening Spring 1997'. He turned away.

'What's the matter?' she asked.

'Nothing, I was hoping to see someone from yesterday.' He took her hand as they crossed the road, they made their way towards the shops and arcades. Everyone seemed to be having a sale, half price this, half price that, they were practically giving stuff away, most of it rubbish, they didn't want any old stock left at the season's end.

They walked down a little side street and in the window of a gift shop they saw a little pot dog in the shape of a spaniel (black of course) carrying a basket of flowers in its mouth.

'Isn't it lovely,' said Angela.

'Come on,' said Jim. 'We will buy it for Doris as a thank you present.'

After it had been wrapped they set off back up the street, he came to the bus shelter, where he had stopped to tie his shoe laces. A cold shiver ran down his spine. It was nothing to do with the weather.

They turned the corner where he'd knocked Angela down. They crossed the road and two little figures caught his eye. He hadn't seen them when they had set off. He bent down to pick them up.

'What are they?' she asked.

'I won them yesterday,' he said shaking the water off the little doll, he squeezed the cuddly toy, it was still sodden from yesterday's rain.

They walked up the steps to the guest house and rang the bell, he hadn't noticed it the night before. To their surprise the woman from the cafe opened the door.

'What can I do for you?' she said, she had tears in her eyes and a handkerchief in her hand.

'Where's Doris?' asked Angela.

'She's inside,' said the woman. 'How do you know her?'

'We stayed here last night.'

'I thought she'd had guests,' said Janice. 'You'd better come in then,' she said standing to one side.

'What's wrong?' said Jim.

'I'm afraid she's dead,' said the woman. 'I'm her daughter Janice. I thought you were the doctor, I phoned a while ago, I was waiting for him.'

'I'm a nurse,' said Angela. 'Would you like me to look at her?'

'Please, if you would.' she said.

They went into the lounge and Doris sat slumped at the table, her head resting on her left forearm, a picture of Julie in her left hand and a photo of Jenny, Peter and Blackie in her right.

'She'd had heart trouble for years,' said Janice. 'I don't know what possessed her to take two guests in after all this time.'

Angela was checking for her pulse, but found none. She held a small make-up mirror to her mouth, but it was obvious she wasn't breathing. She'd been dead for some time.

'I only called round from the cafe to see if she wanted any shopping. I had to let myself in because she didn't answer the door and this is how I found her.'

'I'm so sorry,' said Angela. 'She's been dead for some time now. She took us in last night during the storm, she told us all about her grand-daughter and your sister and brother-in-law being killed.'

'Aye, we wanted her to move to a smaller place after my dad died but she wouldn't, always hoping one day Julie would come back, but that's not going to happen now is it?'

'I don't know about that,' said Jim. 'I think she did come back last night, that's why your mum's gone today.'

Then he told them the story of the day before whilst they waited for the doctor.

THE KISS OF THE SWAN
R D Weaver

Each night, from the wings, Tamara would watch in silent adoration as her idol danced, except of course when she was required on stage herself. It was more than simply admiration for a fellow artiste, a greater artiste than she would ever be. More than hero worship. It was love. A high and spiritual love, she told herself. She had little hope of rising higher in her profession, and would probably have left the company long ago, except that it would take her far away from *her,* for whom she would have gladly lain down her life.

How could she ever confess to such things? Olga Radetskaya was a great prima ballerina, probably the greatest of her day, whilst Tamara was a lowly member of the corps de ballet, scarcely visible to such an ethereal being. Radetskaya was proud, as they all were, but not aloof or cruel: there was a warmth and kindness in her smile and a gentleness of spirit. Of this Tamara could be sure, for she had seen it once, briefly.

It had been the opening night of her first Swan Lake, and Radetskaya was to dance Odette. The Little Swans had clubbed together to buy a gift for their Queen, and to her delight (and also horror) Tamara was elected to make the presentation. It had caused a minor sensation when she had ventured into that area of the wings traditionally reserved for primas. Only her great love could have induced such a timid creature to approach so hallowed a place. Watched by all she had come forward, curtsied, presented her small tribute and said in a whisper 'From all of us Madame, good luck.' The radiance of the Queen, her make-up lending her a strange other-worldly beauty, high and worshipful, was hardly to be born by any earthbound creature. Tamara felt shrunken before her. But Radetskaya smiled gently, and to the astonishment of all the other 'great ones', she leaned forward and kissed her small acolyte.

'The nerve of the creature!' others had exclaimed afterwards.
But Olga Radetskaya had only laughed. 'Nonsense,' she said. 'The poor child meant no harm, and I was very touched by her gesture.'

For Tamara it had been the fateful fairy's kiss that had bound her forever. Something very special had passed between them, something that for a time would sleep, but would soon waken and blossom into something quite unforeseen.

Then had come the accident for which the world of dance has long mourned. Radetskaya's courage during her recovery earned her the respect and love of the world. But her spine was shattered beyond repair, she would never dance again, never walk.

Tamara's heart came close to breaking. She sat by her Queen's bedside and wept long. Since the time of the kiss a friendship had begun to grow between those two. Tamara had meant to leave the ballet and devote her life to Olga's care, but she forbade it. She *must* go on with her dancing. Olga even persuaded her old teacher Madame Karpova to train her young protégé. And although Tamara believed her dancing would now give her no joy, she was determined to work hard if it would give pleasure to Olga Radetskaya, who would always be her Queen, and her friend.

Gradually it became clear, as she trained, that a greater spirit than she had believed she possessed now moved within her. She danced as she had never dreamed she could. Her rise in the Great Company was to be a rapid one. First she was promoted to coryphee, then to soloist and finally to the greatest honour of her profession: prima ballerina. When she made her debut in Swan Lake, there were many who swore they had watched Radetskaya dance once more.

It was only then that Tamara truly recognised the thing which had passed between them with that kiss. In that moment of mutual recognition a Queen had passed on her crown to her successor. Often afterwards as she danced, seeing her reflection in the studio mirror, or even sometimes before an audience, it seemed as if not she but another, greater than her, was dancing. And sometimes it seemed that, as before, she merely watched from the wings as a wondrous creature danced for her adoration. Her body had become the mere vessel of a glorious immortal spirit that could not be crushed or broken, but would dance forever.

STRANGERS ON A TRAIN
Jenny Bosworth

Climbing aboard the train the thought of seeing my parents (or adopted parents) was exciting after my first year at university. To say I was homesick was an understatement.

After the first half an hour of having a carriage to myself, a lady entered. At a guess she was about forty-five years of age and in my mind her dark eyes were her best feature. 'Do you mind me sitting here?'
'No' I answered, 'how far are you travelling?'
'Only ten miles,' she smiled and started reading the paper.

I continued reading my book which was 'Far from the Madding Crowd'. After a few minutes the lady said 'My family are in the news again.'
'Who are they?'
'Kink, my uncle is in Harley Street.'
Kink, that name rings a bell. Wonder where I have heard it before? Failing to think I decided it was best to carry on reading my book.

After a few minutes it came to me. It was my mother's real name, Mary Kink. My adopted parents adopted me as a baby so I never knew my real mother, but I had been told. Could the lady sitting across from me be my real mum?

I have her nose, I thought. Yes, I did resemble her. No, it would be too much of a coincidence. 'My name is Ann by the way.'
'Oh, nice to meet you Ann, I am Mary Chambers.'
She is called Mary and she could have got married. No, it is not possible. 'Was Kink your maiden name?'
'Yes it was.' Mary answered, 'I have been married twice before so I can add Cooper to my list. He died of a heart attack.'
'Sorry to hear that.'
'I'm not' she laughed.
'Did you have a family?'
'No thank God, the only kid I had got adopted.'

For a moment then I hoped she was not my mum. A mum that does not like kids. That was hard to take. Just then the train pulled into a station.

'This is where I get out.' Mary smiled as she got up.

'How old would the child you had adopted be now?' I asked.

'Nineteen, you want to know everything, don't you?'

'Sorry, I did not mean to pry.'

'That's alright. Her name was Ann like yours.'

Mary Chambers said goodbye and I knew she was my mother. I would not miss that few minutes with her for anything.

AUNT POLLY
Collin West

'I came to with the phone seeming to make more clamour than usual. I tumbled out of bed, and looked at the clock, ten to seven! Who on earth could phone so early?'

Aunt Polly had just started telling me about something which had happened before she retired from nursing. She had such a fund - all quite fascinating. 'Why have you stopped? Do please go on.'

After a pause she continued 'I reached for the phone. Hello? And from the reply I suppose my voice said more than I intended!'

'Hello Polly, it sounds as if the first thing I must do is apologise, especially as I'm going to ask a special favour. It's Peter Cass here, and I had to ring you so early in the hope that you would help with an urgent case. It's a lovely child about five. She so desperately needs all the care and attention which I know you can give.

You'll find the father a bit odd' he continued 'he's a Mr Charles Webb and is the senior partner in a big practice of solicitors. Got a pencil handy? I'll give you the address.

Once again I'm sorry to call you so early but the crisis may come at any time and I wanted to get you there as soon as possible. Incidentally, I increased your fee quite considerably, do say you'll go?'
'Of course I will, I just hope I'll be able to help.'
'Splendid, I still remember those one or two near miracles when you were working with me. I'll contact their Dr Lomax and suggest he calls to see you in the late afternoon. I know you'll do all you can, and I'll hope for good news soon.'

There was a long pause and finally I asked 'Who is Peter Cass?'
'He was a well known children's specialist - he only helps in very special cases now. Quite early in my career I admired his care and dedication. I felt the same, and as a consequence a bond of mutual respect was formed between us. It was like old times hearing from him again.'

Aunt Polly seemed to slip into a daydream, then she continued 'I went back up those creaking stairs which as a child had often talked to me. This cottage was where I was born and where I had nursed my mother during her last illness. Those creaking stairs which had said so much to me as a small child gave me confidence, and through the many exams later would creak - 'of course you can do it, get down to it!' Now in retirement I felt at home, and without a doctor in the village I was often able to give a helping hand.

With thoughts of that very ill child still very much on my mind I was soon on my way. When I left the train I was lucky to get the only taxi. As I gave the address the driver gave me a strange stare.
'What's the matter?' I asked
'Rather you than me. You'll understand better when you meet him. What I don't understand is how he manages to have one of the nicest girls working for him.'

The driver insisted on taking my case up the front steps, and as I pushed the bell the sound reverberated throughout the building - I felt quite a chill!

This feeling didn't last long. Maisie opened the door with such a welcoming smile 'You must be the nurse. I'm so terribly glad to see you, Dr Lomax said you would arrive this afternoon; poor dear little Elizabeth is so very ill. Do please help her, this house would be dreadful without her.'

Maisie showed me to my room and brought hot water and also a welcome cup of tea. 'I guessed you would like to freshen up and I thought a cup of tea might help.' She didn't know that Polly was the nick-name I had been given because in any emergency I always wanted a cup of tea.

It didn't take long, and as we went into Elizabeth's room she opened her eyes saying 'Maisie, oh Maisie, you aren't going to leave me are you? What should I do if you did?'
She gave her a hug and said 'Of course not my love, this lovely lady has come to look after you.'

Peter was quite right - a lovely child but so very ill. I immediately told Maisie to bring me fresh sheets, blankets and pillow cases, and a fresh nighty.

'I can't do that' she said 'the master said we had always changed the bedding once a week and that must continue.'

Aunt Polly suddenly stopped.

'Are you still feeling angry?' I asked.

'No, not angry. Looking back, I just think how absurd the whole situation was. At the time I was stunned, I had never been in any similar situation ever before.

After a moment Aunt Polly continued 'Do as I say Maisie and I will take full responsibility. Hasn't the man any sense?' I had just made the necessary changes and got the child comfortable when the doctor arrived.

'What do you think' he said.

'I'll do what I can, but this household! It seems to be slightly mad; I doubt if I can do much.'

'Anyway, you've made a good start,' he said 'Poor Maisie is very worried. I'd love to be a fly on the wall when you meet Mr Webb! I'm glad to have met you. I'll pop in tomorrow.' And he was gone.

When Maisie came in she said 'The master has his evening meal at seven o'clock on the dot, he insists it must be served at the last stroke of the hall clock. I'll pop up and tell you, but please' her voice pleaded, 'be ready.'

Maisie was as good as her word. At the bottom of the stairs I was greeted by Mr Webb. He sailed towards me with a condescending expression which reminded me of a camel looking down in the haughty way they do. He extended his hand. 'I'm Charles Webb, I'm glad you could come at such short notice; personally, I didn't think it was necessary but the specialist whom Lomax called in was adamant. I hope you're as good as he said you are.'

'I will certainly do all I can, but your daughter's condition is very serious indeed. It will need a miracle to pull her through.'

His voice sounded like someone chewing silver paper as he said with heavy sarcasm 'Let's hope you can also work miracles.'

Ignoring his unpleasantness I said 'I'm sure you will agree, but as anything could happen at this time I persuaded Maisie to stay with Elizabeth, and your cook kindly agreed to look after dinner just for tonight.'

His face! What had I said?

'You will kindly confine yourself to looking after Elizabeth. I insist that Maisie should serve dinner; the cook's place is in the kitchen - do I make myself clear?' His tone was icy.

For a moment I wondered if I was hearing correctly, and I replied as coolly as I could 'I had to make these arrangements simply because Elizabeth must not be left. Either I must have full co-operation in trying to save the child's life or I will leave at once. Incidentally, I must also tell you that this afternoon I insisted on a complete change of dry bedding on the child's bed. Although she had a temperature she was cold. I have never in all my experience met anything quite like this.'

'How dare you speak to me in such a manner. And in my own house!'

By now I was really angry. 'Then it is high time someone did. It is this absurdly silly attitude of yours which will probably make the difference between life and death to your child. I'll have no part of it; if you will excuse me I will phone for a taxi.'

I was just going to ask the exchange for the number when he came out, and replacing the ear piece he said 'You are right. I just didn't realise. For so many years I have had to insist on everyone doing as I said, and quite wrongly I carried this over to the situation here. I hope you will forgive me for my rudeness, do please stay. Do whatever you feel is necessary. I suppose I don't show it, but Elizabeth means so very much to me.'

I understood the generous effort this proud man had made to speak as he had done, and my anger was gradually replaced by admiration. There were one or two things which I wanted to put right, but felt it wise to wait!

We went back and finished the meal in silence, and I was impressed with the way the cook helped in what had become a difficult situation.

Going upstairs I tried to calm myself. Elizabeth was restless when I went in, all she kept saying was 'Where's Maisie, I want Maisie, don't send her away will you?'

Finally she seemed satisfied with my continual assurance that Maisie would stay, and lay back dozing on and off.

It must have been around midnight when Elizabeth became very restless. She tossed and turned, threw off the bed clothes, sat up, then just as suddenly, laid down. I bent over the bed and held her close trying to quieten her. Then quite suddenly she became very still and completely stiff in my arms, reminding me of the times when as a small child I held my dolls. She stared unblinkingly, wide-eyed, at the foot of the bed. I glanced across and saw a beautiful woman standing there watching my every move. I was struck most forcibly by her powerful piercing eyes which held Elizabeth's stare. Instinctively I waited with the growing feeling that this was no ordinary occurrence; rather in some way outside the normal.'

I looked at Aunt Polly. She had always seemed such a down to earth person; what was she talking about? 'What do you mean?' I asked.

'It does seem very extreme,' she said 'maybe a bit potty I know, but that feeling continued with me for a very long time. Was there more in that happening than just me and the child? By this time Elizabeth was already in a deep sleep, and without looking, I somehow knew the lady had left the room.

*   *   *   *   *

Immediately I enter the breakfast room, Mr Webb looked up with what was supposed to be an inquiring smile! - 'How is Elizabeth?'

'She is in a long, healing sleep, and I'm sure she will make a full recovery.'

'I do hope you're right,' and then suddenly as if remembering, he said 'of course she will.'

I broke the silence which followed, saying 'A beautiful woman came into the room last night. It was during Elizabeth's crisis, her eyes opened very wide, and she stared straight into the piercing eyes of the lady at the foot of the bed.'

For a few seconds he had a look of utter disbelief. Finally he became the man I had known the night before, anger and disbelief showed clearly on his face. 'What do you mean?' he asked coldly. 'There is no such person in this house.'

'Nevertheless,' I insisted, 'it was so, and as their eyes met I am certain some communication was made. At that moment Elizabeth's body was completely straight and stiff like a board, but immediately the look passed between them, she became relaxed.'

'I have never heard such ridiculous nonsense, it's just not possible! Describe her,' he said tersely.

'You will appreciate I was fully occupied with Elizabeth, and the incident could only have lasted a few seconds; even so, I am absolutely certain that my description is accurate. The lady was tall and slim, the dress she was wearing was dark red, with very pretty flowers worked on both sides of a white collar: it was drawn in at the waist with a belt about a foot wide in the same material and I noticed how perfectly it fitted. She just stood and stared at the child.'

As I watched every drop of blood drain slowly from his face, and the heavy lines stood out even more starkly in its ghastly whiteness. He put his head in his hands and trying hard to stifle a deep-throated sob he said in an awesome whisper, 'That was my wife, she died three years ago this month.'

I sat back and stared at Aunt Polly. 'That is the strangest story you have ever told me,' I said. 'Do you really believe it?'

'Sometimes I wonder if it was me' said Aunt Polly 'but I assure you it happened just as I said. One other thing: watching the pain and sorrow of this haughty man, all my own feelings evaporated. I began to have some inkling why he was as he was. He must have loved her so desperately, that somehow in a strange, twisted way he had blamed the child for her death.

With a deep sadness in my heart I went quietly upstairs, and after making sure that Elizabeth was still in her healing sleep, started to pack.'